Praise for
DANIELLA CARMI'S
Samir and Yonatan

P9-CER-089

■ "The bitter suffering of a Palestinian family is at the center of this moving novel, eloquently translated from the Hebrew. . . . with the message, there's the moving drama of individual kids who become friends and help each other through pain when they get a chance to know each other." —*Booklist,* boxed review

"Young teens will relate to Samir's feelings of being an outsider and will appreciate the message of peace that is the central theme of the book." —*VOYA*

"An Israeli author debuts in English on this side of the Atlantic with a sad but not heavy tale of life and death on the West Bank. . . . This hospital story will leave readers pondering the resilience of children in the face of tragedy." —*Kirkus Reviews*

"Life in the hospital is described as clearly as life in the Occupied Territories and readers will sympathize with Samir's fear and loneliness and welcome his new friendships." —*School Library Journal*

Winner of the 2001 Mildred L. Batchelder Award
For Best Translated Novel

A 2001 Notable Book for a Global Society

UNESCO Prize for Children's Literature in the Service of Tolerance,
Honorable Mention

Other Signature Titles

Ghost Cats
Susan Shreve

Midnight Magic
Avi

The Firework-Maker's Daughter
Philip Pullman

A Hive for the Honeybee
Soinbhe Lally

The Music of Dolphins
Karen Hesse

Tangerine
Edward Bloor

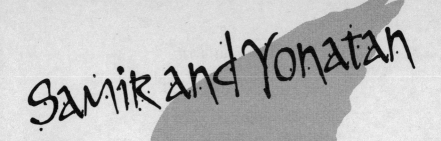

Samir and Yonatan

by Daniella Carmi

translated by Yael Lotan

SCHOLASTIC INC.

NEW YORK TORONTO LONDON AUCKLAND SYDNEY

MEXICO CITY NEW DELHI HONG KONG BUENOS AIRES

To my children:
Galia Liliane, Michal,
and Tom

No part of this publication may be reproduced, stored in a retrieval system, or
transmitted in any form or by any means, electronic, mechanical, photocopying,
recording, or otherwise, without written permission of the publisher. For
information regarding permission, write to Scholastic Inc., Attention:
Permissions Department, 557 Broadway, New York, NY 10012.

Arthur A. Levine Books English hardcover edition was designed by
Elizabeth B. Parisi and edited by Zehava Cohn, and was published by
Arthur A. Levine Books, an imprint of Scholastic Inc., March 2000.

ISBN-13: 978-0-439-13523-8
ISBN-10: 0-439-13523-0

Text copyright © 1994 by Daniella Carmi.
Translation copyright © 2000 by Yael Lotan.

23 22 21 20 19 18 17 16 15 14 13 12   7 8 9 10 11 12/0

Printed in the U.S.A.   40

First Scholastic paperback printing, January 2002

One

Since morning I've been waiting for a curfew. If there's curfew I won't be able to leave the village and won't have to travel with Mom to the Jews' hospital. So, like a chicken, I'm perched on the windowsill, waiting. Sure enough, it has turned out to be a quiet day. The street's empty. The *sahlab* seller is walking down the road, dragging his sick leg. I wouldn't mind dragging my leg like that old man all my life, as long as I don't have to go to the hospital.

I can't remember the street so quiet. And today of all days. A bus arrives. People get off and walk quietly down the street. Not a single army jeep roars into the neighborhood and stops with a screech, and nobody's running in the alleys. Even the air is clear today. No smell of burning rubber.

Far off I see Adnan, my friend, kicking a torn tennis ball. Dribbling it neatly till he gets to my window, he leaves a cloud of dust behind.

"Anything going on in the market?" I ask, full of hope.

"This morning there were burning tires near the square," Adnan says. He pulls a green apple out of his pocket and takes a huge bite.

What's the use of tires that burned this morning? I think, watching Adnan chewing, and I know that he's already been through the market and helped himself to some rotting fruit.

"Want to come?" he asks, and spits out the piece of apple. I point to my bandaged leg, but Adnan is not impressed. What's so impressive about falling off a bicycle on the market steps? Though I'd felt great when I rode down the wide stairs from the bakery to the pitta-bread seller. I'd never dared before to take that shortcut down the market steps with all the pittas. It was the first time I did it. I remember exactly what I said in my heart. I said: Your brother Fadi would do this with a smile on his lips. I said: Now hold your breath and ride down like the devil. But even while the shops flew past and the wind was hitting my face, I knew that I'd never be like my brother Fadi. The brave ones die. Cowards stay alive. . . .

Sometimes I have a strange thought. I think: if I'd only got a bullet in the leg, instead of falling off the bike like a fool. I can see myself returning from the hospital on crutches, limping on one leg. The only leg I've got left. An empty pant leg, flapping in the wind. I enter the class. The teacher stands up. Somebody claps. . . .

"They're playing soccer in the alley," Adnan says, bouncing the ball low and catching it in a round palm, like a sports star on television. As if they had ever let me be goalie when my leg was all right. Adnan notices my sour puss. "Without your brother Fadi, the game's no good anyway," he says, and slips away from my grudge like a hair pulled out of bread dough, and soon he's dribbling down the alley.

The 4:15 train whistles as it comes near, and Grandpa goes out into the yard. It's an old habit of his. When we were little, Grandpa used to come out a minute before the train and round us up, so we wouldn't play near the tracks. The fence has been broken for years and there's nobody to fix it. Grandpa always stands close to the train, to feel the wind on his body. I look at his face the moment when the train is opposite the house. His face goes hard in a strange way. As if he'd jumped on the train and was already gone beyond the mountains, to faraway places.

Grandpa is blind. In the evening he and I watch the news from Jordan or from Egypt. The news announcer tells us about battles in Yugoslavia. Grandpa listens and I describe to him how people are getting on trains and running away from bombed cities. Then they sit on their suitcases in railroad stations or schoolrooms in strange countries. The old women cry. The children try to sleep on benches. I once asked Grandpa which side is right in that war, and he snapped, "You can be sure of one thing — everybody thinks he's right."

Here comes another bus. Mom gets down with the bags and walks quickly. Soon she'll put up the rice to cook, then she'll be ready to go to the hospital. I listen as hard as I can. I think I can hear somebody screaming in the side street, but it's only a crow. Again I pray for a couple of jeeps to drive through, fast — these days they always drive at least two by two — then for the sound of people running down the alley. Please, God, I beg, it's been such a long time since I asked for anything . . .

Grandpa sits on the *mastaba*, smoking, and for once my sister Nawar, who never stops talking, is as silent as a rock while she washes the rice. I remember when they used to stuff cabbage leaves or zucchini with the rice, and there was gravy and I think sometimes meat too, but I'm not sure about that. Never seen her working like this, not my sister Nawar. Suddenly she's a busy bee.

Maybe if she started to talk about the guy she met in Bethlehem, and what he said to her and what she said to him, she'd never finish. She always talks about him as if he's still alive. From telling the story she'd go on to complain, and from complaining to swearing that she'll never ever marry our cousin Rashid, because he's just a waiter and she's a high-school graduate. And nobody would say a word, until Dad would burst out of his silence and yell that the live one is alive and the dead one is dead. Then Nawar would start crying and Grandpa would start pinching his cheeks, and with a bit of luck we'd be too late for the bus. Maybe they'd even put off this trip to the hospital, maybe even drop the whole idea.

But now, like a hostage, I stand at the bus stop between Mom and Dad, leaning on the crutches. Dad waits with us, and meanwhile he checks the crossing permit that Mom got through the lady lawyer she works for. It's a special permit for an operation at the Jews' hospital. Mom could have slept for three nights on the steps of the Administration and never managed to get such a permit. But here comes the bus. It's never been this early.

Two

"Take your pants off," says the doctor, while a nurse stands there, looking on. Mom's gone to pick up some X rays from another room. On the walls are huge pictures of landscapes, with water splashing from snowy mountains, like in the movies. I'm perched on the bed like a goose at the butcher's. I pretend I don't understand.

"Pants off, please," he says in Jews' Arabic, looking at me as if I'm his only son. He closes the curtain around the bed, so I can be alone, and I undo the button, get tangled with the zipper, and then let the pants fall down to my shoes. I don't make a move. I'm waiting. It's awfully quiet.

A radio is playing faraway music. The doctor says a few words to the nurse, almost in whispers. Here everything is quiet and nobody's in a hurry. The doctor comes in through the curtain, but leaves the nurse outside. I thank him for it in my heart. He takes the bandage off carefully. He's got white hands, like the priest in that Saturday night program on Jordan TV. Mom comes back with the X rays and the doctor looks at them against the light. He invites Mom to sit down, but she remains standing. He tells her the knee bone is shattered, that they'll have to wait for the expert doctor from Chicago. Until then, he says, I should stay here.

In the picture, the water keeps rushing down the mountain under a blue sky without any clouds, but inside me my heart is dead. I shut my eyes, listening to the quiet. Now the whole world's wiped out and I'm left alone in this room with the blue light that hums. I'm scared and a little confused, so I let them do what they like with me. They lay me down on a high bed with wheels and a male nurse in a white coat drives me down long corridors. I'd like to sit up and look back, to see if Mom's coming after me, but I stay lying down. We go up and down in elevators; the ceilings are shiny white. Inside my stomach there's something pressing, as if they stuffed a heavy stone in there. . . .

"Easy, easy," says a fat nurse and grabs me under the arms. The male nurse takes my good leg, and together they heave me into a bed in one of the rooms. I'm so confused. I don't see the room or the other beds or the kids lying in them. I see Mom. She sits down on the bed, but the nurse makes her get up and brings her a chair. Then she — the nurse, I mean — waters the plants on the windowsill beside me, humming in a voice like a singer. Mom shrinks in the chair. She whispers, "You'll wait here for the doctor from America, Samir."

Why so quiet? Maybe talking isn't allowed here? How can she leave me alone in the Jews' hospital? I want to shout, but I'm woozy from the examinations and the X rays, and my knee's on fire. Mom puts a few apples in the drawer of the bedside table, and I feel the rope tightening around my neck.

I don't even remember the moment Mom leaves. I close my eyes and the silence soon swallows me up. I sink into deep sleep. In the silence I hear the voice of Bassam, my older brother: "Open the door, Mom. . . ." For a moment it's like Bassam is bringing in a crate of vegetables, but there's something not right in his voice. "Mom, open the door. . . ." Doors are opened and slammed. Shutters are closed. Bassam and a friend of his bring in my brother Fadi wrapped up in a blanket. They lay him on the table. I hear Grandpa coming out of the room, yelling, "What happened? What happened?" There's a big bloodstain on the end of the blanket. Mom closes the shutters, going from window to window, making the whole world dark, so there won't be a bit of light left.

"Do you like red jelly . . . ?" The fat nurse is bending over me; she smells of a strong perfume. She places a tray with food on the bed and fixes the pillow under my head.

"You know why the jelly's shaking, Samir?" Strange that she's talking to me like we know each other. "It's scared that you'll swallow it." She laughs. I stare at her pudgy arms. I'm afraid to move.

"What's this? You put it in the bed again?" she asks the kid in the opposite bed. "What am I to do with you, Tzahi?" The boy called Tzahi sits up with a jump and takes the tray from her.

"Do me a favor, take it out of there," she says. There's a bulge under his blanket beside his legs.

What's he got in there? A rooster? A puppy? He

looks a couple of years older than me. Anyway, his hands are enormous.

"You hear me?" the nurse insists, but Tzahi is sipping his soup, making funny noises with his mouth. The kids laugh out loud.

"Why do they always give us these choking cakes, Vardina?" Tzahi asks the nurse, encouraged by the laughing. He picks up a piece of cake and shows it to everyone. "So dry it sticks in the throat." He crumbles it in his hand and laughs.

But the nurse speaks to the boy in the bed next to mine. "Take a break, Yonatan, won't you?" He's absorbed in a book. He looks like he doesn't hear anything. When the nurse puts the tray in front of him, he sticks a pencil between the pages and closes the book. He's got a big watch on his wrist, the kind with a panel of buttons. There's an iron contraption on his other hand, so he can't move it.

He says to Tzahi, "There are galaxies flying away from us at two-hundred million m.p.h."

I look to see what Tzahi will say to this, and he — just as soon as the nurse turns away — stands up on his bed and starts to bounce like a billy goat.

"Cool!" he says. Yonatan is not impressed. He eats

his soup. He has short fair hair, like the soft fuzz on a chick, and a thin braid hanging down his back. He eats quietly, while Tzahi rocks the bedsprings.

"What's your name?" asks a pale girl with a bandage on her forehead.

Her bed is far from mine, near the door. I don't know if she is talking to me.

"His name is Samir," says the nurse, and Tzahi sits down with a hop.

"Samirrrrr!" Tzahi says, drinking the soup straight from the bowl, making noises like he swallowed a frog. "His name is Samirrrr!"

In the grocery where I worked in the summer they weren't too crazy about my name either. The shopkeeper asked me if I'd mind if he called me Sesame. That's what they called the boy who worked there before me. Why should I mind? It's not like it's my real name. It's only a name for the Jews' grocery.

"I'm Razia," says the girl with the bandage in the far bed.

Awfully skinny, this Razia. In the bed beside her lies a girl with fair curls. On the windowsill behind her she has a row of teddy bears and dolls. She looks like a doll herself and doesn't say a word.

I eat the chicken so fast I hardly taste it. They forgot to salt it, but that doesn't bother me. They mashed the potatoes into a kind of baby porridge. Maybe that's why I finished them so quickly. There's also a red sauce that I don't know what to do with, so I drink it straight from the bowl. I'm so hungry, my ears are twitching. I swallowed up everything, and now I wish they had added a pitta. The fat nurse asks if I want seconds. I don't know what it means, but I say yes, and she brings me the same tray, only without the red sauce.

Everybody's eating. Only the girl with the golden curls who looks like a doll doesn't touch her food. She lies there looking at the window, not saying a word. Like a baby — lying there and petting a stuffed rabbit. A girl who looks at least twelve.

"Shall I bring you a yogurt, Ludmilla?" the nurse Vardina asks. "You must eat something. . . ." Ludmilla doesn't move; it's as if she can't see her. "If you don't eat, we'll have to connect you to tubes," the nurse says.

What sort of tubes is she talking about? Like a watering hose? I'm thinking that after the nurse leaves, maybe I'll go and take Ludmilla's tray.

"Your body needs fluids." The nurse speaks to her like a mother. "You don't want it to dry up, do you?"

She makes a sign to Razia to give Ludmilla the soup. Razia hands the cup of soup to Ludmilla, but she makes no move to take it.

"She wants to be breast-fed, like a baby," says Tzahi.

"She is not a baby," Vardina replies. "She knows that her body needs liquids. . . ."

"Her body is a mass of complex and elaborate molecules!" declares Yonatan.

For a moment everybody falls silent, as if deep in thought. Ludmilla pets the rabbit, and it reminds me of the she-rabbit that my little brother Fadi got from the bakery after working there for two weeks. We used to give her leaves that we collected in the market at the end of the day. The rabbit knew she belonged to Fadi; she followed him everywhere.

The nurse takes Ludmilla's tray, puts it on the cart, and goes out. I'd like to get up and follow the cart, at least hold on to the smell, but I don't dare. Tzahi takes a brand-new soccer ball from under his blanket and starts to run and dribble it between the beds. "Cool!" he shouts. I think about my friend Adnan running in the alleys right now. I wonder who got to be goalie. The dusty alleys and the square and the market seem so far away. I bet they've forgotten my name, I think to myself. I picture Adnan escaping from the soldiers, running through the alleys and giving them the slip. . . .

"Catch!" Tzahi shouts and throws the ball. It lands right on my injured knee. I double up with pain, trying as hard as I can not to scream, but my knee is like a bushfire. I pull the cover over my head . . .

Three

"Good morning, Samir. Would you like to bathe?"
Nurse Vardina comes so close that she might as well
be in my bed, drowning me in her perfume. She herself always looks like she's just come out of the bath-
house. Her smock is always white. Her shoes are
white. Shoelaces — white. I don't feel an urgent need
to wash. If it was up to me, I'd just go on lying here,
not moving a finger. I remember last night, how I
tried to turn over without screaming in pain. I want
them to forget me. But the nurse grabs me and pulls
me up and hands me the crutches, and I hobble
through the room after her. The other kids are still
dozing. Only Yonatan has already got his nose in a
book. He is wide awake. When I pass by his bed, he
raises his head to look.

The shower room looks brand-new, like they just finished building it. The walls are covered with shiny, greenish tiles, as is the floor and the ceiling. There's a little recess in the wall for soap, and on the soap there's a picture of a girl with a fish tail instead of legs. A brand-new, pretty, blue soap. Nobody's used it yet.

The nurse wants to help me take off my pants. I hold on and don't let go.

"Are you embarrassed in front of me?" She laughs her thick laugh. "I've already taken down the pants of ministers and prime ministers," she says, and peels my pants off quickly. Then she wraps the bandage with a special covering so it won't get wet, while I'm standing in front of her on one leg like a stork. Don't know what to do.

I'm not taking off my shorts, I say to myself. Not if they skin me alive!

The nurse urges, "Come on then," and tries to strip me naked.

"No. . . ." My voice sounds peculiar in Hebrew.

"What, no?" she laughs. If only she didn't laugh. I'd rather she yelled. Her laugh hurts more than slaps. I hold on to my underpants with a clenched fist.

"You want me to go out?" she asks.

I'm so ashamed, I can't say a word.

"All right," she says, "but please scrub your neck and also behind your ears." She cuts off a length of sponge and gives it to me.

What does she think I am, a baby? For a moment I pray that Mom will come in with the loofah and say in her quiet voice, "Come, let me scrub your back before they cut off the water."

At last the nurse goes out and I start to scrub. The sponge is soft, not like a loofah. I'm not even sure this sponge can get dirt off. I'm so jumpy, I keep scrubbing my good leg, as if that's all that's left of my body. What if I really end up with just one leg? I've heard of such cases that couldn't be cured and it had to be cut off. I'd be walking on crutches all my life. Like the sahlab seller who doesn't have the money to get an artificial leg. I'd never be able to run. Never fly down the alley feeling the wind in my face. I'd get used to sitting at home. These days, if you can't run you'd better stay home. As for soccer, forget it! I see myself limping on crutches in the market. Going down the wide stairs. Passing by a group of tourists. They look at me in silence. They think it happened from a bullet in the leg. Let them think so; I keep my mouth shut.

They look at me and I don't say a word. I'm silent, like real heroes are silent. . . .

The door opens and the nurse comes in with a towel. "Why just the leg?" she scolds. "I see you need help after all."

"No . . . ," I croak, and freeze. I stop right there. Not moving. Hardly breathing.

"Do you want Nurse Felix?" she asks, her voice suddenly soft. Maybe she can see my cutoff leg.

I should have told them right from the start that I don't want to shower today. It's just that everything here is so complicated. It's hard to say yes and it's hard to say no.

Somebody's knocking hard on the door, like the soldiers do before a search. I'm waiting for him to burst in, but he opens the door a crack and peeps in. He looks like a smiling goat.

Doesn't look anything like a soldier, this Nurse Felix. He's got a red nose like a clown. He soaps the sponge and hands it to me, running his eyes all over me. He doesn't seem to care about this wash at all. Allah knows what he's thinking about, this Felix, when he soaps my back carefully all over.

Afterward, he wraps me in the towel. Doesn't notice that my leg's still soapy. I don't care either. He hugs me with the towel, drying me and laughing. I ask myself, what would your friends say if they saw you now? What would Dad say, if he saw how they look after you like a mother?

In the nights, Dad sat in the kitchen, silent. Nights were when he used to do the barbershop accounts. Not that there was ever a lot of work, Dad says, it was never a big business. A little barbershop for men at the far end of the market. Couple of chairs, that's all. But these days all the shops close every other day, on account of the situation. So a week's work isn't what it used to be. And that's not counting the costs, or the taxes, which keep going up and up. Anyway, who gets a haircut at the barber's these days? People get haircuts at home. They cut each other's hair.

People have nothing to do during the curfew, Dad says, so they give each other haircuts. He can't even remember the last time somebody came in for a shampoo or a shave. I go and sit beside him in the kitchen, but he stays silent. Sometimes I think that since Fadi died, I don't exist much for Dad either.

FOUR

In the morning three doctors come and examine my knee. They look at it from all sides and look at X rays and talk to one another, but don't say a word to me. I thought at first they were doctors from America, because they are talking in English. I can't understand what they are saying. All I know in English are sentences that I remember from the beginning of the Aladdin story, which I learned in school two years ago. They go like this:

"Once there was a wizard. He lived in Africa. He went to China to get a lamp."

We never got to learn the rest of the story, because just then they arrested our English teacher and he hasn't come back since. But I'm holding on to these three sentences; I repeat them to myself every night so

I won't forget. If I forgot these three sentences I'd have no English left. Some nights I'm so tired I don't have the strength; I'm half asleep, but I still force myself to repeat them quietly, under the blanket. Adnan says they might work against the evil eye. I'm not really sure, but how can you tell?

The doctors put a contraption on my knee and tell me not to get out of bed. Finally Vardina comes in and tells me that the doctor from America will arrive soon, and then they will do the operation. I lie without moving and think how the hours here pass so quietly, as if there's no world outside, and soon they'll bring another meal.

Tzahi keeps running around, as if there's nothing wrong with him — till Vardina and Felix come and draw the curtain around his bed and do something to him that I can't see. Yesterday I did see this thing, but I don't know what it is. Every few hours they come to Tzahi and shut themselves in there with him, and then the room goes all quiet. Everybody stops what they're doing. Even Yonatan closes his book and looks restless. They all lie still, waiting for something. Allah knows what. Only when Felix comes out with a bowl covered with a towel, and Vardina opens the curtain and smiles at us as if nothing happened — only then do the kids begin to act normal again. And each time Yonatan, as soon as it's over, puts on his slippers and goes to the toilet. I stare at Tzahi — we all stare at Tzahi — but you can't tell anything by the way he looks. Right away he has to do something naughty. He'll go and spit into Vardina's flowerpots, or put on Ludmilla's pink housecoat and walk around with his hands in the pockets — walking like a pasha's son, as Grandpa would say.

We don't have much time to look at Tzahi, because Vardina comes in and tells Razia that her father wants to visit her.

Razia gets up without a word and starts to tidy her bed — tucking in the sheet and arranging the pillows — even though Vardina says it isn't her job to do this, and that everything will be done for her, the sheet will be changed and all. Razia doesn't seem to hear her. Vardina talks to her in a loud voice and calls her by name, but Razia has turned to stone. She sits on her bed, doesn't move, and doesn't make a sound. Then all at once she pulls out the sheet, throws off the pillows, and messes up all her neatness. Then she crawls under the bed and sits there with her head on her knees, as if all the troubles in the world are after her. And no matter how people beg her to come out and call her name, Razia doesn't budge.

After a while Felix shows up. He looks like a soft talker, and everybody starts calling, "Felix, Felix, come to me. . . ." But Felix is busy with Razia. When she doesn't answer him, he doesn't mind crawling and joining her under the bed. He stays there with her for some time.

That doesn't help much either. Razia only starts to cry softly, and doesn't calm down even when Felix blows up a balloon for her. Vardina looks into the room and says to Felix, "If she's crying, that's already something." In the end they promise Razia that her father will put off his visit, and Felix gets her to come out and cry on her bed.

Everybody lies quietly, looking at Razia, and I wait for her to stop crying. I guess I've gotten used to this place where nobody runs and nobody yells, and there's no noise or shots or smoke, where the room is bright with blue fluorescent light, and the air is warm like in the hothouse my uncle used to have. You could go in there without a shirt even in winter. And in the corridor, a radio is always playing faraway music, and outside the window there's a tree with birds in it. . . .

Pretty soon I have to go to the toilet, and don't know how to get there. The doctors told me I wasn't to get out of bed, and even took away my crutches. I lie on my bed, waiting and waiting, watching Ludmilla pet her rabbit. I'm thinking that she doesn't eat and she looks like a princess, the daughter of the Caliph of Baghdad, and the Caliph would give her food tray to anyone who would cure her of her illness.

In the end I can't wait. I get off the bed and start to hop on my good leg. I just make it to the corridor when Vardina appears out of nowhere and makes me lean on her shoulder. She says I'm lucky the doctors didn't see me, and starts to take me back to the room. I hate to pass Tzahi's bed like this, with her arm around me, and I'm trying to remember how to say it in Hebrew — I mean, when you have to go.

"If you need the toilet, just press this button," Vardina says, tucking the blanket around me. "They'll bring you a bedpan."

I look at Tzahi's bed. I hope he didn't hear. That's all I need, for Tzahi to see me using a bedpan. But after another hour I can't stand it anymore. I press the button and close my eyes and wait. Felix comes in with a bedpan and draws the curtain around the bed. Just for that I'd kiss the ground under his feet, as Grandpa would say. I'm not even ashamed when he helps me sit up and hands me the pan, because he pulls, out of my ear — honestly, out of my ear, I swear by the Prophet's beard! — a red balloon. Right away he blows it up and hangs it on my bed.

When night comes, I can't fall asleep. My thoughts keep running around, like my feet used to do. I try to turn from side to side. The side facing the room is already hurting, so I try to turn on the side facing the window without bothering my knee. I work so hard with my head and arms that I break out in a sweat. When at last I manage to turn over and lie facing the window, I see Yonatan standing there. He's standing on a chair, looking out of the wide window at the black night. Suddenly, he turns to me and says in a clear voice:

"You know that the Milky Way looks like the backbone of the night?"

I'm so surprised to hear him talking to me, I don't know what to say. He opened his mouth and talked only to me. My soul escapes a little and flies over the bed. I don't understand exactly what he's saying. I know it has to do with the stars, because that's what he has in his book — pictures of all kinds of faraway stars. I'd like to ask him a question, but don't know what. There's such a lot of questions you can ask about the stars. Maybe more than stars. But Yonatan stands and keeps looking out the window as if he doesn't expect an answer. And that's how I fell asleep, looking with this downy boy at the stars. It's been a long time since I saw them, because in our place nobody likes to go out at night, and if you must, you certainly don't look up at the sky. But here the stars twinkle at you from the night, and when you shut your eyes you go on seeing them. They fly closer and closer till they fall down on you.

Five

In the morning I was awakened by a police siren and wanted to jump out of bed. Only my leg, which is heavier now with the contraption they put on it, pinned me to the bed and reminded me that I'm in the Jews' hospital, waiting for the doctor from America to come and operate on me. In the meantime I get to eat three meals a day, which they bring to my bed on a tray.

The sound of a siren comes from the radio. In a minute somebody changes stations, and again there is the soft, dozy music that plays here all the time. I peep at Yonatan's bed. He's lying there, deep in a book. I give a little cough. He doesn't turn his head. I think for a moment that maybe I dreamed what he said to me last night, when only the two of us were awake. He shows no sign that anything happened.

Vardina comes to give him his breakfast. He takes the tray without looking at it and asks her, "Do you know why the earth is round?"

"Why?" she asks.

"Because it's rotating all the time, and that compresses it and makes everything round."

"I see," says Vardina. "Please eat your egg today."

I think that if he doesn't want his egg, maybe I can help him with it. But he peels it without thinking and eats it without noticing, and all the time his nose is deep in his book.

I swallow my breakfast before I can taste it, and think that now all I have to do is wait for the next meal. So I pull the blanket over my head and stay like this for a while, because it bugs me to see Ludmilla lying with her tray in front of her, not moving, while the food is getting spoiled.

Under the blanket, thoughts about Fadi always come to me. It started last year, in the winter. Right after Fadi was killed. There were cold winds. I could see the pigeons huddling among the leaves of the neighbors' tree. I thought about the rain trickling into the cold ground. It happened again in the spring. Our whole yard was a muddy mess, and the sun couldn't dry the puddles. So when the seasons change, thoughts about Fadi come back. To drive them away, I quietly repeat the morning prayer, which is also good against the evil eye: "Once there was a wizard. He lived in Africa. He went to China to get a lamp." But even while I'm saying this pretend prayer, I feel my body drying up; it will soon turn to stone. I hope someone will come into the room before the next meal and make the time pass more quickly.

Sometimes I see a man with a yarmulke going down the corridor. He wears white pajamas and has a biggish belly, and he sings to himself: "*Yiboneh bais hamikdosh . . . bimheira beyomainu. . . .*" Something like that. He trills his voice, drawing out the words. Sometimes he comes into our room, Room Six, and takes a few steps as far as the window, singing all the time. He stops for a few seconds beside each bed. I don't know what to do when he stops in front of my bed. He actually has a nice voice, but I don't know what his job is. I wonder if he's trying to tell me something and if I need to answer, and also if he goes like this through all the rooms. The children are not surprised by him at all. They hardly look at him. He could be a nurse who's come in to take our temperatures, or something.

Yesterday a sister of Tzahi's came to visit. She was

wearing high heels and carrying a basket full of bags of peanuts and candy, which Tzahi kept rustling for ages. She went from bed to bed and gave some to each of the children. Me too. She offered me a bag and I looked at her red fingernails and wanted to take a huge handful of peanuts, but before I could think about it, I heard my voice saying "No." Maybe I was feeling shy. But no, I didn't really want it. What's the use? I want Mom to come and bring me almond pastries and sweet sesame bars, like we used to have when I was small. But it doesn't matter. She doesn't have to. She could simply come without bringing anything. Just come. As for Dad — I can't picture him coming to visit me, not even in my dreams.

I start to torment myself in my thoughts. I say: If it was Fadi lying here instead, Dad would come. And he would talk. But there was a time when Dad also talked to me. That was before he went into this silence of his. We used to chat about the old Volkswagen, when it was still working. Little chats made up of short sentences, just the two of us. He would tell me about his worries: if the car was eating up oil, if it would pass the test. Now it's standing in the empty lot full of bullet holes — ever since the day when somebody thought it was the car of a collaborator, and finished it off. Dad took out the engine and sold it for pennies. Only the body of the car remains, like a big useless insect. Little kids climb into it and pretend they're driving away.

Yonatan's father came yesterday. He's tall, with long curls hanging down to his shoulders. I thought at first he was Yonatan's sister. He sat on the bed and talked quietly. Yonatan asked questions out of the book and his father answered, almost in whispers. Tzahi ran around laughing, "Yonatan's father works in the stars. . . ." I'd be awfully happy if my father worked in the stars, or whatever it is. The stars are always there. Even in hard times. Stars don't vanish when there's curfew.

This is how I talk to myself. Very slowly, I go over every member of the family: Grandpa sitting all day long on the mastaba, smoking, with Mom telling him that the cigarettes are making him shrivel up. Bassam working in Kuwait, no one hearing from him anymore. Suddenly I think I can even stand my sister Nawar — even though she hit me when I looked in the napkin where she keeps a curl from that young man from Bethlehem, the one who she said was on the wanted list. I can hardly believe what's happening to me, if after a few days away from home I'm already thinking good thoughts about my sister Nawar.

This morning a woman who is not Razia's mother, and is not a nurse came to see her. The woman drew the curtain and we all lay quietly, doing nothing. Even Tzahi stopped running around and sat on his bed, though he kept making faces at the rest of us. But he soon stopped that after a while, and when we began to understand from the talk what had happened to Razia, we became silent. One night, Razia's father drank too much arrack, and he hit Razia in the forehead; since then she has a wound there. But now, the woman says, the father wants to visit his daughter, and he's begging her to believe him that he didn't know what he was doing that night.

We heard the woman talking and talking behind the curtain. We couldn't hear Razia. Then the woman waited a little while, and said that the father will wait patiently till Razia agrees to let him visit. In the meantime, Razia can be as angry as she likes. There was a silence. We didn't say anything either, though I was surprised that a father has to get permission from his daughter to come and visit her. Still, I didn't say anything. The woman opened the curtain and went away. When they brought in the ten o'clock tea, Razia gave Ludmilla her cup, as always. Suddenly, Ludmilla sat up and drank the tea and even ate a cookie.

All day long I watch Yonatan, but nothing happens. He goes on reading his book and doing sums on his watch, which is also a calculator. Only in the evening, when I'm not expecting anything, does something happen again. I am feeling sleepy, but I still have a cookie left from supper that I am sucking on slowly, to make it last. Everyone else is already asleep. Felix, who's on the night shift, passes with his flashlight from bed to bed, looking at us. I ask him if he is counting us, like my brother Bassam told me they do in jail, before lights-out to check that nobody's escaped. But Felix says that he is going over the beds to make sure that everybody is off to the Land of Nod. Then, after he turns off the lights and goes out, it happens again. Yonatan talks to me in the dark. I can't see his face, but his voice is bright and clear.

"Want to come with me to the planet Mars?" Just like that. Simple. Just like Adnan asks, "Want to come with me to look for Marlboro stubs?"

My head starts to spin. I don't know what to say.

"I can't walk . . . ," I mumble.

"I know," says Yonatan.

I'm hoping he doesn't think I'm chicken or something. Maybe I look chicken, which is what Adnan and the others think. But I'm not. It's just that since what-happened-to-Fadi, Mom doesn't let me go to the market or the square, and Dad locks the door when the sun goes down. The other kids call me "Rabbit," but I think that a rabbit isn't brave — but isn't a coward either. All it's got is speed. It doesn't have hoofs, it doesn't have sharp claws so it runs away. That's all. I don't know why it suddenly matters to me that this downy boy shouldn't think that I'm scared to go with him on a long journey, or Allah knows where.

"We'll have to wait till after the operation," Yonatan says, as if he's been thinking about this business for a long time.

"Right . . . ," I squeak. I don't really know what I am saying.

"Right . . . ," Yonatan repeats, and then I see that he has been standing on his bed and looking at me the whole time. "Till after the operation," he says in that clear voice of his. It amazes me that he is speaking about it as if it's his operation, as if he's waiting for it with me.

Six

Today after supper there was a power failure. A little lightbulb remained burning in the corridor, but our room was in darkness, and everybody sat on their beds in silence. A moment before it happened, Tzahi was running around with the ball. Then he froze — and the ball rolled off and stopped under one of the beds.

I'm used to these sudden darknesses. We often have electricity cutoffs at home. Mostly they happen when there's a curfew on, I don't know why. Just when everybody is shut in at home and the television is on, suddenly there's darkness which joins the silence in the streets. Then we're all even more alone with our thoughts. I see Grandpa's cigarette glowing bright and then pale again. But it's all the same to Grandpa — to him it's always dark.

Yonatan starts talking fast. As if the darkness is his great chance, a chance that may not come back: "Think what it would be like if we counted all the grains of sand on earth," he starts by saying.

"What for?" asks Razia.

"Because if we could do this impossible thing, maybe we'd get an idea of how many stars there are in the universe — because the number of stars is bigger than the number of grains of sand on earth."

Nobody says anything. Then Tzahi jumps up: "How do you know? You haven't counted them!" I can hear him grinning.

I'm a bit sorry for Yonatan, because that Tzahi is sometimes dumber than my shoes. But I don't say anything. And Yonatan just goes on — as if to say that the dogs bark, but the caravan moves on — sailing off to his faraway stars. He describes the creatures that he's sure live out there, and talks about distant worlds that nobody's ever heard of — worlds made of ice and gases and rocks and red sands and black oceans, worlds surrounded by marvelous colorful rings, glittering like gems. And all these worlds, he says, are waiting for us. Just for us.

I'd like to believe him, but it isn't easy. My friend Adnan also likes to tell fancy stories, and in the end you find out that it all grew inside his head, and everything is made up.

Like once he told me that the mute chicken seller had a pistol in the box that he sits on, and that one day we should go past when he's busy with a customer, pick up the box, grab the pistol, and run away. The dummy won't even be able to yell for help, Adnan said. So then we hung around him for maybe half a day, and he watched us and got to know every move we made. He might have been mute, but he wasn't blind. He never took his eyes off us for all those hours. Then a friend of his, a big strong guy, came and sat beside him, and the chicken seller made coffee for him and kept him there. I'm sure it's on account of us that he kept him there for almost a whole hour. Kind of signaling to us that he was not a little beardless child, that we shouldn't think we could trick him. It felt like Adnan wanted to quit, but by then he didn't know how. In the end the chicken seller picked up the box — as if to show us (I'll swear by my father it was meant for us) — and showed the big guy all the little chicks he keeps inside.

But the kids in the room seem to believe Yonatan's stories. They've been quiet for some time. Maybe each one is thinking about his or her chances of getting to one of those stars. Anyhow, suddenly there's something serious in the air. Like the time for foolishness is over, and now we're talking seriously. Or maybe it's because of the dark, because all at once I hear Tzahi saying: "My problem is, I can't pee. So they put in a tube, and the tube's connected to a nylon bag, and when the bag is full they empty it and finish. That's all. It's just until I get well."

You'd think the kids would feel mixed up by the story of this illness, something you never even heard of, but Yonatan isn't, not for a moment. He goes on in the same voice, as if he's still talking about those stars, but now it's as if he's a doctor in a white coat. He says: "It's just until you can pee in the normal way."

And Tzahi says, "Exactly," as if a great weight has rolled off his heart.

Then Razia starts to speak out of the darkness like Yonatan: "If my father could stop drinking and get well — maybe he'll be able to pass the night in the normal way."

And Tzahi says again, "Exactly," and quickly brings us back to himself, so we won't forget: "If anyone wants to see, I'm ready to show the bag that the urine goes into."

Yonatan and Razia run barefoot to Tzahi's bed.

They sit there with him and I hear them whispering and laughing. Then Tzahi goes to Ludmilla's bed and says to her, "You can touch it, if you like."

I can't see what she's doing, but Tzahi asks her patiently, "You want to touch it again?" And Ludmilla says in a weak voice, "Enough." It's the first word I've ever heard that girl say. Then I hear Yonatan whispering to Tzahi, "Samir hasn't touched it yet."

Tzahi says, "So what?"

Yonatan whispers, "It's his turn now."

But Tzahi doesn't answer. He just climbs up on his bed and jumps up and down, making the springs creak.

Yonatan insists, "Why not?" but Tzahi goes on jumping. And now, like a dummy, I do awfully want to touch that stupid bag of his.

At night I dream that Ludmilla is sitting on a princess' throne, and her father, the Caliph, gets mad at her silence and hits her on the forehead. Then the soldiers come and arrest Ludmilla and take her in for questioning. But she is silent, refusing to say a word, and does not betray her father. The Caliph then realizes his daughter's heroism and begs her to forgive him.

Seven

Every morning, even before they take temperatures and before Vardina brings in breakfast, Tzahi pulls the curtain around his bed. Then the children get out of their beds and go to look at his bag and to touch it. Tzahi lets them in behind the curtain, but only one by one, never two together. I hear them whispering and giggling behind the curtain. All very softly. The others wait patiently outside the curtain. The one inside always wants to stay longer. I hear Tzahi saying, "All right, Razia, that's enough. Go out now. The others want to come in."

Razia begs, "When my dad comes and brings some salt peanuts, I'll give you some."

"Okay," Tzahi says, "but go out now."

The only one he doesn't try to rush is Ludmilla. He

lets her stay as long as she likes. But the trouble is, she doesn't like to touch the bag, not Ludmilla. She just goes in and right away she wants to leave. Her voice sounds like a princess who's going to faint any minute.

Tzahi tries to get her to stay a bit longer. "But you just came in!" he says.

"Enough," says Ludmilla. She leaves and goes back to her bed like the daughter of a proud pasha. This girl is tearing Tzahi's heart.

The staff also gives her special treatment, this Ludmilla. Vardina sits with her at every meal. She takes a yogurt for herself and eats beside Ludmilla, to help her swallow. "One more spoon," Vardina says, putting it in her mouth, and waits for Ludmilla to put one in her own mouth. "One last spoonful . . ."

"I'm not hungry . . . ," Ludmilla sighs.

"Never mind," says Vardina. "You're not eating for yourself now, you're eating for me."

Never saw such a thing in all my life. And this is a girl who looks about twelve, and keeps petting her stuffed rabbit.

Yonatan, when Tzahi lets him behind the curtain, asks a lot of questions. I think he enjoys the questions more than touching the bag. I hear him asking questions like a doctor, and tossing sums around, until

Tzahi gets fed up and tells him he won't let him in again.

Tonight, for the first time since I came here, I talk to Yonatan. He's standing on a chair, like he does every night before going to sleep, looking at the stars. For a long time I don't dare bother him. It isn't easy to start talking about something that's not connected to stars. Maybe he won't like it. And when I try to open my mouth, the words won't come out.

Here, in the Jews' hospital, I almost never say a word, even though I understand almost everything in Hebrew because I worked in that grocery. Anyone seeing me here must think that I'm a really silent type.

After Fadi died, I decided that I'd never speak again. I sat on the windowsill and heard the aunts wailing and thought I'd sit there and never budge and never speak again. I said to myself: Let them come and try to make me get off. Let them come, let them beg. I won't get off and I won't speak. I'll just sit here on the window like a statue. I'll never ever let myself get off this window. Because if I move away, it'll be as if the world can begin to forget Fadi. . . . I sat there all night, and by morning I couldn't feel my body, it was so stiff. I thought if somebody pushed me with a little finger I'd drop outside like a stuffed sack. I didn't even go to the funeral. Only at noon, when Mom returned from there, and gave me a look, then I knew I had to get off the window.

Just now — I don't know what for — I ask Yonatan why his mother doesn't come to visit him. He doesn't answer for a while, then he speaks without looking at me.

"My mother doesn't live with us," he says. "She lives in the United States." But he doesn't sound like he's unhappy or anything, even though he doesn't have any brothers. He and his father live alone at home. Still, he doesn't sound sad. Now I understand why his father grew such long hair — maybe so he can be a mother to Yonatan as well.

"Why doesn't anybody come to visit you?" Yonatan asks.

"It's too far," I tell him. I can't let him think that they forgot me, so I try to bring up every excuse for them: "Dad has to keep the barbershop open till late. Because if anybody does come in for a haircut, it will be in the evening, after work."

"And your mother?" he asks.

"Mom works as a cleaner in a lawyers' office in town. And when she has the strength, she also works the night shift in a bakery."

"Then she must bring you fresh bread in the morning," says Yonatan.

"Pitta," I say. "Once she brought a roll with sesame seeds."

"I bet the roll your mother brought you was fresh from the oven," says Yonatan.

"It was."

"I bet it was the freshest thing in the world, the roll your mother brought you," he says.

I think that Yonatan would like to go on talking about my mom. It takes me no time to realize that he doesn't like to talk about his own mother. He prefers to talk about his father — how his father goes everywhere on a bicycle, and has rubber bands to fasten his pant legs so they won't get caught in the chain. Then when he gets to work he puts the rubber band on his hair and ties it into a kind of ponytail.

Yonatan's dad teaches about stars. But not to children. Grown-ups come and he shows them the stars and teaches them. That's his job. The way somebody else washes dishes in a restaurant and somebody else bakes pittas and another is a barber in a barbershop, Yonatan's dad gets up in the morning and goes to tell people about what's going on in the stars. They even pay him money to do that.

Eight

I wake up this morning to see Tzahi running around the room, shouting, "Chocolate crispies!" There are two young women with yellow hair in the room. One has braids and her name is Ingrid, but the other has a difficult name, so Tzahi said we should call them Ingrid One and Ingrid Two. Ingrid One and Ingrid Two can't speak Hebrew or Arabic. They smile and talk to us in Norwegian. They bring a little cart into the room with a small hot plate, a pot, and bowls with grayish grains that I've never seen before.

Ingrid One melts the chocolate in the pot, and Ingrid Two invites the children to come and stir it. Tzahi jumps up and rushes to be first. He grabs the wooden spoon and starts to push it around wildly. Ingrid shows him that this is not the way to stir. She shows him how to do it with round movements. Then it's time to add butter to the chocolate. Tzahi right away cuts off a piece of butter, but Ingrid Two wants someone else to add the butter to the chocolate, and invites Razia to do it.

Razia slips the butter into the chocolate and stirs it in. In the meantime, Ingrid One tries to get Yonatan to put away his book. But Yonatan won't pay attention; he's too interested in his stars. Ingrid One and Ingrid Two bring the cart up to Yonatan's bed, so he won't have to get up, but Yonatan creeps deeper into his book, like a worm in an apple. They pass on to Ludmilla, and all the time they try to calm Tzahi, who keeps running around the pot with the spoon in his hand, spattering chocolate.

They want Ludmilla to pour the grains into the chocolate. Ludmilla sits up in the corner of her bed and stares at the grains with wide-open eyes. Her eyes are blue, like the sky on a bright day. I can tell she'd really like to do it, this Ludmilla. I can see she wants to, only somebody forbade her to touch food. Somebody cast a spell on her. . . . I slip under the blanket and repeat my three sentences against the evil eye. It's quiet. I close my eyes and open them again. I see Ludmilla pouring the grains into the chocolate. Her

face is serious, as if she's carrying out a sacred duty —
except that her tongue sticks out of her mouth when
she pours all the grains into the pot. It's a real miracle.
Ludmilla gets out of bed and follows Ingrids One and
Two and the cart. Now they come to my bed.

They give me little paper cups and show me how
to separate them one from the other. I separate them
carefully and put them on a tray, and Ludmilla fills
each cup with a few grains coated in chocolate. I put
down a cup and Ludmilla pours. I put down another,
and she pours. I arrange the cups in rows on the tray,
and Ludmilla pours carefully, so that not even one
grain falls outside the cups. I never did anything so
nice in all my life. I'm cooking with Princess Ludmilla,
after freeing her from the spell. Her eyes are blue and
quiet, like the sea, which I've never seen. And all this
in the Jews' hospital.

Fadi's rabbit had red eyes. When she died, the
eyes stayed open and their color became purple. Fadi
said it was from the tear gas. But the neighbors' goat,
which they keep on the roof, didn't die, even though
tear-gas grenades fell near her several times. Her eyes
stayed brown. Maybe goats are more resistant to

these things, Fadi said. Or maybe it's because she's got milk inside her body, and that protects her. He started to ask Mom for milk, day after day. But there was never enough. We used to sneak up to the neighbor's roof, me and Fadi, to take a little milk from the goat. We didn't know who we were more scared of — the neighbor, or the soldiers who could suddenly rush into the alley and spot suspicious movement on the roof.

I'm lying in bed, eating the chocolate crispies that Ingrid and Ingrid cooled for us in the fridge for a couple of hours. They crackle in my mouth, making a nice sound. I remember the packet of chocolate that Bassam brought to me and Fadi. We kept it for some time, till Fadi said we should bury it with the rabbit, so she wouldn't be all alone in there.

I wish I'd put something for Fadi in his grave. I'm sure that if I'd died, Fadi wouldn't have forgotten to put something there for me. . . .

Sometimes I wake up yelling from a dream. Vardina comes and brings me some liquid for sleep, and after that some raspberry soda in a glass, to take away the taste. That raspberry drives away all my bad dreams. When I get back home I'll tell Grandpa about it. Raspberry — that's what he should drink every night when he can't fall asleep. I drink the raspberry and look at Vardina, who's standing and waiting for me to finish. I'd like to ask her when someone will come to visit me — but I'm not sure if Vardina is the person to whom I should ask such questions.

Nine

I don't remember how we fell asleep, but we wake up to hear Tzahi noisily chewing the candies his sister brought him. He crunches them aloud and says: "These are sour balls — lemon-flavored. These are orange, grapefruit, tangerine . . . These are chewies — strawberry, raspberry, cherry . . . These are mint — they cool my breath. Ooh, it's cold inside my mouth! Ice, snow, hail . . ."

We sit up and watch Tzahi, and listen to the noises he's making in his mouth. We can almost taste those candies on our tongues.

"Who likes licorice candy?" Tzahi asks, but doesn't wait for an answer. He takes a long brown stick and puts it in his mouth, sucks it, then opens his mouth wide to show us. His mouth is like a black oven after it baked pittas all day long. He laughs, and his teeth shine like the fire in the oven.

Tzahi says, "Cool!" and the rest of us sit with our mouths open, not moving or breathing. We all hope that Tzahi will throw us a candy, but he doesn't throw a single one, just sits and chews them in front of our faces and laughs. We sit around, watching him roll his tongue, crunching one candy after another with his teeth, until he finishes all but one, which he lays on his bedside table. Then he blows up the empty paper bag, thumps it with his fist, and the bag bursts noisily.

Suddenly, I see Ludmilla getting out of bed. She steps into her embroidered slippers. You'd swear that only Princess Scheherazade or somebody like that could have such slippers — little white shoes embroidered with silver. The Caliph of Baghdad would order such slippers to be made for his daughter. She goes up to Tzahi's bed and stands very close to him: She doesn't say a word, only opens her mouth and sticks out her tongue. Tzahi takes the last candy — I don't know if it was lemon or raspberry or a cool mint — and quickly peels off the wrapper, which he throws on the floor. The sound of the paper alone gives me goose bumps. The candy is very colorful —

orange with yellow and green circles, like a funny sort of fruit that's been cut open to show the insides. Never saw such candy. Tzahi puts it on Ludmilla's tongue, and they both laugh. I'm thinking to myself that maybe my magic won't work on Ludmilla anymore.

At night I wait for Yonatan, but he doesn't get up. I can hear his breathing in the bed next to mine and I know he's gone to sleep. I lie alone, staring at the wide window and looking for stars. But the sky is cloudy. Somebody's covered the stars with a kind of dirty blanket, and I can't see anything.

Suddenly I hear Tzahi getting up and moving around the room barefoot. I try to lie very still. I listen. But Tzahi must have heard some movement from my bed and he comes over, then stands beside me and looks at me. I keep my eyes shut and try not to breathe. I don't even know why. I don't know why I'm afraid to look in his eyes. But Tzahi knows that I'm awake. He grins, saying, "I know you're not asleep, Samirrrr. . . ."

I open my eyes and look at him.

"You know that my brother is a soldier?"

I don't know what to say to him.

He's serious now. The grin is gone from his face. I

don't feel very well with Tzahi standing right in front of me not moving. It's as if he's saying, "What will you do now?" In my mind I repeat the three magic sentences. Tzahi looks at me for a few more seconds, then moves away and gets into bed. I lie without moving, listening to his breathing. I'm not so scared of what he said about his brother. I'm more scared of his voice and of the darkness, and how we are suddenly alone in the room. I'm trying to picture Tzahi's brother, and I see a tall guy in army uniform with a helmet on his head. I can't see his face.

Since what-happened-to-Fadi, I don't tell Grandpa when I see soldiers. Even when they're on television, I stop telling him what's going on. Even if it's something happening in a faraway country, I make it short and say as little as possible, so as not to upset him. Because Grandpa gets upset by every little shot. It doesn't matter if it's happening in the neighbor's house or in Africa.

"I hear shots," Grandpa says to me, and moves closer to the television to hear better. "Where are they coming from?" he asks.

"Far away, Grandpa," I say. "Africa or someplace."

"South Africa?"

"Far away, Grandpa," I tell him.

"Tell me what's happening."

"A battle between whites and blacks," I say.

"The whites are shooting? Allah destroy them."

"It's hard to see who's shooting," I say, trying to calm him.

But Grandpa is starting to pace restlessly around the television, and Mom makes me a sign to try harder.

"There, they are scattering . . . ," I say with an effort.

"Scattering what?" Grandpa gets mad. "The whites and the blacks? All lining up in rows and breaking up quietly, hey? So why can I hear shots?!"

"They're all going back . . . to their homes," I mumble. But Grandpa sits down on the mastaba and starts to pinch his own cheeks. After that he usually lights one cigarette with another, all evening long. In the end he'll shrivel up from the smoke, like Mom says.

Dad says Grandpa has no friends left. Some died. Some became too religious. And of those who are left, there isn't one that Grandpa hasn't gotten mad at during an argument, yelling at him that he's a prize donkey.

"If you swim against the current, the water will sweep you away," Dad says to Grandpa.

And Grandpa replies: "And if you sail with the current, you'll get lost."

I never know why all of a sudden they start talking like a pair of fishermen.

Ten

Tzahi shouts: "The paratroopers are coming!"

I wake up in the morning and see Tzahi standing on his bed looking at me. It looks as though he's been standing there a long time, waiting for me to wake up. "The paratroopers are coming!" he yells again. Then he takes a flying leap off the bed and starts to run around in the room. The breakfast tray is on my bedside table. There is a roll, which I like. But I feel that this morning I'm not going to enjoy the roll. Not even the sour cream. The night is still turning around in my head like a black cloud.

Tzahi goes up to Yonatan's bed and shows him an emblem that he has stuck to his pajamas. "My brother's coming to see me today," he says to Yonatan. "He's a paratrooper."

Yonatan reads out loud from his book: "The temperature on Venus gets as high as 380 degrees Celsius."

Tzahi says, "Cool!" but doesn't seem to care. He climbs back on his bed and begins to jump up and down, looking at me. I don't know why. Yonatan raises his head and tries to talk to him.

"It's a regular little hell, that planet Venus," he says. He looks as if the terrible heat on some distant planet is tearing his heart worse than anything that can happen in this room. He turns to me and says, "This planet of ours could have been a real paradise. All the conditions are here. . . ." He smiles at me like we're friends.

Tzahi says again, "My brother is coming to see me today!" Then he jumps straight from his bed onto Yonatan's. Yonatan doesn't seem to mind. I'm beginning to feel a little sick. I swallow a bite of the roll and it sinks like a rock into my stomach. I can't put another thing into my mouth.

Yonatan starts to explain why this earth is so wonderful. "The sun warms it neither too much nor too little, and there is rain, and plants that give us oxygen. And so many kinds of animals have evolved here on earth, so many species and types. Just think how many beetles and insects are hanging around in the forests, and how many fishes and creatures live in the sea! But they'll still be there only if we don't spoil this world for ourselves and for the people who will come after us. . . ."

But Tzahi couldn't care less about all the bugs and fishes. He jumps back into his own bed, takes the soccer ball from under the blanket and starts kicking it at the legs of the beds. "My brother got his wings," he says, as if his brother is a much more wonderful animal than all of Yonatan's beetles and fishes, and he wants Yonatan to know it. I picture Tzahi's brother jumping from a jeep and suddenly taking off and flying like a big bird over the village lanes. And all the time Tzahi comes closer to my bed, kicking the ball in my direction. I can already feel the explosion he is going to set off in my knee.

"Whales," says Yonatan. He gets up and talks straight at Tzahi, trying to catch his eye. "Just think — such gigantic creatures and so intelligent. And they are all mammals like us, our own family."

"In our family, everyone's a paratrooper," says Tzahi, and throws the ball to Razia. Razia throws it to Ludmilla, and Ludmilla throws it back to Tzahi.

Then Tzahi throws it back to Ludmilla, and the ball hits a flowerpot on the windowsill and knocks it down. It smashes on the floor.

Vardina comes into the room. "What happened?" she asks. Her voice is dry, not a bit like when she sings. "What happened?" she asks again, looking at us. Her eyes pass from one to the next. Nobody answers. Tzahi sits on his bed, crossing his arms calmly, with a kind of smile on his face — the patient smile of a camel, as if he'd never touched a ball in his life. Razia giggles, but she's frightened, and Ludmilla stares at Vardina with big eyes, blue as the sky, then starts to cry softly. "Who did this?" Vardina asks, and tries to gather the dirt back into the broken pot. Ludmilla's weeping just gets on her nerves.

"We got this plant as a gift from the mother of a boy who was seriously ill, who was our patient here. It was a souvenir. To me, no other plant can take the place of this one, because when I water it every morning I think about that child," she says sadly.

I see Tzahi's face turning pale. The smile has left his lips. Ludmilla cries harder.

"You're allowed to do whatever you like here. You are pampered. You're indulged. And this is the thanks we get!" In the end she looks straight at me, and her look is worse than a beating.

I don't know what to do. The fear that I woke up with is taking over. I'd like to point at Tzahi, so that everyone will know exactly who the criminal was. I'd like them to punish Tzahi, to pull him out of this room like a weed out of a vegetable patch. And I'm also scared. Scared of the hate that's gripping me by the throat and choking me. I want to calm myself down. I'd like to put a spell on everybody in the room so that everything could go back to the way it was. Then I could slip under the blanket and eat the roll with the cream. I thought that this place was outside the world, that no troubles can come after me here. I repeat in my mind the three magic sentences: "Once there was a wizard . . ." But it doesn't help.

Yonatan pipes up: "We all did it, Vardina." He's playing with his braid with his fingers. He stands facing Vardina, like a baby chick raising its head. His voice sounds inside me like a bell. Vardina looks at him, surprised. She holds the plant, which sticks out of a ball of dirt between her hands, and stares at Yonatan — as if he'd appeared suddenly and solved a mysterious riddle. Ludmilla stops crying all at once.

Tzahi stays on his bed, not moving, just looking down at the floor. Everybody starts to breathe properly again. I didn't know that anybody could be such a saint in this world. I didn't know such a thing existed. I want to kiss Yonatan. Vardina's anger is gone, as if somebody poured a bucket of water on her.

"The plant will be all right," she says. "I'll transfer it to another pot." Then she walks slowly out of the room.

Eleven

Tzahi's brother shows up at noon. He is in uniform, but without a helmet on his head. His hair is mussed and he looks more like a kid who forgot to comb his hair than a soldier. He lays his rifle in the corner under Tzahi's bed, sits on the chair, stretches out his long legs, and yawns. He looks as if he could fall asleep on the spot if they let him. He doesn't have any wings.

Tzahi sits on his brother's knees and pats him all over, as if he isn't sure that he's real and here in this room. He touches everything his brother has, this Tzahi. Touches and pats him all the time. He unbuttons his pockets, takes out a bus ticket, a comb, and all kinds of papers, which he looks at very carefully, one by one, laying them one on top of the other. He patiently smoothes out the wrinkled ones. Then he puts them back in a little packet into the shirt pocket. His brother lets him do whatever he wants.

But he keeps the comb, this Tzahi. Then his brother suddenly remembers that his hair is mussed and goes to the mirror over the sink, wets the comb, and combs his hair. Now, with the hair stuck to his forehead, he looks even more like a kid. Tzahi also wants to comb his hair with a wet comb. He smoothes the hair down one side and then the other, and can't decide which side to comb down. His brother takes the comb and pastes Tzahi's hair down on his forehead, too, and now they look even more alike than before. They could be twins.

Tzahi's brother sits in the chair and stretches out his legs again, and now you can really see how tired he is. His eyes almost fall shut. Tzahi comes and sits on the bed facing him and gives him the comb. The brother takes a piece of paper from his pocket, wraps it over the comb, and begins to play the saddest tune I ever heard. His hands shake a little when he plays. I don't know if it's because he's tired, or the effort of playing. I never saw one of these soldiers so close up and without a helmet. . . .

Tzahi's brother takes a cardboard box out of his knapsack, opens it, and gives it to Tzahi. Then Tzahi pulls out a slice of sweet *knafeh* with his huge fingers and eats it. The smell knocks me over. I remember that I hardly tasted anything all day, after the night with Tzahi. But still my stomach feels heavy, almost blocked shut. I can't put in a crumb. Tzahi stuffs his mouth and his brother sits there, enjoying the sight of him chewing. Suddenly I see the cover of the cardboard box and it falls on me like a blow. SHEHADEH & SON, it says. Shehadeh, from the town near our village.

All at once I can't wait anymore for Mom to come. I can't go on pretending that I'm okay without any of them. I can't hold back from asking Vardina when they will come to visit me. I have to ask her right away. This minute. I press the button for the bell and don't stop.

Vardina comes running in. "What happened? Why are you ringing like mad?" she asks.

They all look at me, and I feel too bad to say a word.

"What's happened to you? I'm in the middle of doctors' rounds!" Vardina says angrily. "You need the bedpan or what?"

Tzahi's brother raises his head and looks at me. Tzahi grins. I hide under the blanket, and Vardina leaves.

In the dark I can see Dad sitting very still. He doesn't turn on the television. He has shut the blinds and is sitting in the dark. Mom is doing the washing in the kitchen, and Dad is sitting on a chair in front of Grandpa, not saying a word. Grandpa is smoking as usual. After all, it's always dark to him. Nawar comes in and wants to turn on the light, but she doesn't dare. Dad and Grandpa are sitting in the darkness. I wait and listen. Maybe they'll say a few words. But they stay silent. Now and then one of them takes a sip of coffee, then puts the little cup down on the tray, and then it's all quiet again.

"Why isn't Daddy talking anymore?" I ask Mom in the kitchen. Mom goes on washing. Her hands rub obstinately, speaking more than her lips. "When a man has had his life stolen from him," she says, "he has nothing left to say."

I want to ask if it was me who stole his life from him. I'm not sure I understand what she means, but I must find out if it's me who did it to him.

*   *   *

At four, Ingrid One and Ingrid Two come in and hand out tea and cookies. Right away, Tzahi offers to help them serve. His brother has left, and Tzahi is quieter today than I've ever seen him. He puts a cup of tea on my bedside table but stuffs my cookies into his pocket, then goes back to the cart and gives the Ingrids One and Two a smile like an angel. They're pretty cut off from what's going on here, these Norwegian girls. They can't even guess what this Tzahi is doing. They look just like those UN soldiers who smile at you, smoking their Marlboros, and don't have any idea what's going on. The Ingrids especially love Yonatan. They stop beside his bed like two little girls, and Yonatan tells them that for four billion years there was only algae in this world. Not that they understand what he's talking about, but Yonatan shows them pictures in his book and talks about big numbers. They pat his fuzzy head and smile, while Tzahi gobbles down everybody's cookies.

Twelve

I woke up in the morning and knew that something was wrong. I had a headache above my eyes, as if I didn't sleep all night but lay there thinking with my eyes shut. I shouldn't say "thinking." Maybe I was dreaming. I saw sights — for instance, Tzahi's brother had grown wings and was flying over the shop Shehadeh and Son. He was a big bird with crushed wet feathers, and in his beak he held a cardboard box with warm knafeh. He flew over the market square in our village, then landed on Tzahi's bed. Tzahi — who also had wings and a beak — and he both pecked at the knafeh and laughed. Then it hit me like a blow to the head: Perhaps it was Tzahi's brother who did it to my brother Fadi, with his rifle.

Ever since the idea came to me, I haven't been able to get it out of my head. Tzahi keeps running in his pajamas all around the room, cheering himself by yelling, "The paratroopers are coming!" And every time he passes and looks at me, I see the look in his eyes and I know that he knows what I'm thinking, and I can't stop thinking it. This thought is turning in my belly like a snake. It's freezing me alive.

Yonatan reads aloud from his book about how for four billion years there was no life at all on earth. It all happened in the last half a billion years, he says. For four billion years there was only algae in the seas and oceans on the face of the earth. Apparently, it's a lot harder for more serious creatures to develop. It took all that long, long time before even the simplest creatures could begin to live in the water. First there were only tiny little creatures that you can't even see with the naked eye, and only after an awfully long time came corals, starfish, octopuses, and cuttle-fish — all kinds of animals I never heard about in all my life — then one of them grew lungs, and began to try to get out on land for a bit, and only a long time after that did life begin to develop on land.

I look at Yonatan and I wonder: Is it possible that

he doesn't see anything? Is it possible that he doesn't see what Tzahi and I see and understand? But maybe he really does see, and even better than we do.

Ludmilla again won't eat or drink. This morning they connected a tube to her arm that goes up to a bag that hangs over her bed. There's a liquid that keeps dripping from it all the time, going into her body. Felix came in this morning when Ludmilla was sleeping and told us that she came from Russia, where she had friends and a school and different customs, and she was finding it hard to adjust. The other children talk to Felix and he advises them how to help her and how to talk to her. But I'm thinking that Ludmilla is the daughter of the Caliph, and only I know that a bad spell was put on her.

I hide under the blanket and try my magic sentences. I say them three times, and the third time I hold my breath from the first word to the last. Ludmilla goes on sleeping. She sleeps almost the whole time now. Maybe she's already too weak. And me, I'm not sure I can still do magic, now that bad thoughts have poisoned my magic powers.

Vardina brings in lunch. I'd like to ask her about Mom, but by now I don't dare to look at her. I'm afraid she'll see everything in my eyes. I'm afraid she'll see Tzahi's brother running with a gun through the market square and the kids running away. Only Fadi stays in the square. Only Fadi does not come home.

"What's with those eyes?" Vardina asks.

I'm afraid to move. Now she can see. I know. She and I know that she can see. She puts her hand on my forehead and right away sticks a thermometer in my mouth. I have a temperature. The doctor who looks like the priest in the television series on Jordan TV comes to see me. He talks with another, younger doctor. They both examine my knee again and again. They look at the X rays. The doctor from the series shines a flashlight in my eye. I'm sure he can see something there. He moves to the other eye and back again to the first. He can see something there, but I don't know what it is.

Adnan used to say that one day all the bad guys will fall down into a deep, deep pit full of snakes. It'll be impossible to save them once they fall in. And every evening, before the sun goes down, Satan plays with them in that pit. Then he shuts it up, smokes a *narghile,* and goes to sleep. Anyone who falls into that pit will never ever be able to climb out again. The trouble is, nobody can be sure they're not one of the bad guys, because it isn't only people who do bad things — it's also those who have bad thoughts. That's right. A lot of those who fall into the pit never even dreamed that they were the bad guys. It's something you don't realize when it happens to you.

But what can I do? I can't stop thinking! I can't stop picturing Tzahi's brother firing his rifle, then hanging it on his shoulder and driving in his jeep to Shehadeh and Son to eat knafeh.

The doctor asks if something is bothering me. I take a deep breath and ask about Mom. I don't mind asking him. I'm not afraid he'll think I'm a coward. The doctor goes off to ask at the nurses' station. When he comes back I can tell by his face that something is not right. He tells me that the territories have been sealed off for some days.

I don't understand exactly what that means, I only know it's bad. I get under the blanket and say to myself, There you are, your punishment has already arrived. And this is just the start — the snake pit will come later.

Felix comes and takes the blanket off my face. He explains what's happening. He speaks softly, as he always does. Coming from him, things don't sound so bad. The roads are blocked and Mom can't come to see me. Such things have happened before, and he believes it will pass. He believes it won't be long now. But inside my head, I can't stop thinking about Tzahi's brother.

Dad takes the blanket off Fadi's face and looks. They don't let me and Nawar come into the room. My big brother Bassam sits in the kitchen with us. Nobody's watching Mom to make sure she won't go into the room. She's lying in bed, and the aunties are trying to get her to take a few sips of *kinnar*. Through the kitchen door I can see Dad lifting the blanket and looking. I can't see Fadi. The chair's hiding him. The end of the blanket with the stain is all I can see from a distance. . . .

Thirteen

The rest of the kids are sleeping when the doctor from America shows up. I was also half asleep, when all of a sudden I saw a man bending over me, chewing gum. Felix peeped over his shoulder and told me that he's the surgeon from Chicago who came here by plane. Now I notice how quiet it is in the ward. People are asleep in the other rooms too, and the doctor woke me in the middle of the night. I guess that's how it is with American doctors, because there it's day when here it's night. The doctor himself looks perfectly normal. He is dressed in ordinary clothes and has about ten pens in his pocket. While he's examining me, he talks to me in English and smiles, just like the doctors in the series about a hospital that they show on Mondays on Jordan television. There too they smile at every patient as if he or she is their only child.

But Felix, who shows him some papers and X rays, is very serious, not like he usually is during the day. Maybe because he has to speak English with the doctor. The doctor asks Felix to tell me that he will operate on my knee tomorrow. I get very excited, thinking that maybe the day after tomorrow I'll be going home. I want to ask who will come to fetch me, and what about the roadblock. But Felix makes a sign for me to be quiet, so the doctor can go on with the examination.

I watch him touching my legs with his thin fingers. He's got hands like a young woman's. I think that this man flew all the way from America to save my knee, and I plan to say "Thank you!" in English to him and maybe some other polite words, after that long journey. Also, I'm afraid because he'll put me to sleep. I think if I could have a few quiet words with him maybe he will do it extra carefully. But what can I say — "Once there was a wizard"?

When he leaves the room, I see that he has on his feet exactly the same kind of wooden slippers that one of the doctors in that TV series has, so I begin to think that maybe he came directly from there just to operate on me.

Felix stays with me and tells me that I won't have breakfast in the morning, because the stomach must be empty before they put you under anesthetic. Right away I feel awfully hungry, as if I haven't eaten for three days. He makes me a cup of tea and gives me a pill to swallow, and stays with me a little. But all the time I am thinking about food. He starts to explain to me how they anesthetize you, putting you in such a deep sleep that you don't feel anything, how you're like a person floating in another world. He is really serious, not like the Felix we usually see, and it makes me think that Felix himself is scared of the operation and the anesthetic. He isn't going to pull any balloons out of my ear. Now the whole business begins to look terribly dangerous, and I sit there with a wonderful taste in my mouth, the taste of *labaneh* balls in olive oil, like Mom makes when Dad gets paid for barbering some UNRWA people. The taste doesn't leave me. Felix wants to explain to me exactly what happens at every moment of the operation, but the pill he gave me makes me feel as happy as a baby, and I don't want to start talking in Hebrew, especially not with the taste of labaneh in my mouth.

In the morning I didn't get any food, only sat in bed and watched the other kids eating. Everything looked tastier than ever. I saw Tzahi put half a tomato into his mouth, the juice running down his chin. Yonatan ate his egg, like he always does, with his nose in the book while his mouth was chewing. The crumbs that fell on the pages he gathered up with his fingers and put in his mouth, and I bet he didn't even taste what he was eating. But I still felt the taste of Mom's labaneh balls in my mouth. No matter what I did, I couldn't drive away the taste — or maybe I should say, my longing for the taste.

Razia ate a roll, which is what I like best of all for breakfast. Even more than the freshest pitta straight from the oven, and more than any other food they give you in this hospital. If I could choose a dish that I could eat every day of my life, I'd choose a roll with sour cream.

In the middle of the day, Yonatan spoke to me. It was the first time that he talked to me this way — not at night, out of the darkness. He came over to my bed and talked to me. I don't know if it was an accident that Tzahi had gone for some examination, and Razia was in the shower. Only Ludmilla was in the room, but she didn't move and it looked like she wasn't aware of what was going on around her. She just lay there, looking at the window, and I kept thinking that I had to find some new magic spell, but nothing came to me.

"When you come back from your operation, we'll go to Mars," Yonatan whispers. "I talked about it with Vardina. They'll give you a wheelchair till your leg gets better."

I stare at him and can't believe it. He looks so serious, standing there and looking at me in his quiet way, this boy. How does he think we'll go there? In a wheelchair?

But I don't ask. I like it when he talks like a friend, whispering a secret just between the two of us. I'm not going to spoil it, no way.

"Together we're two boys with three legs and three hands," he says, indicating his arm that is stuck in the contraption. His good hand plays with his thin braid. "I've made all the calculations," he says. But when Tzahi comes back to the room, Yonatan falls silent and dives into his book, and I start thinking my own thoughts. I get under the blanket and picture how we'd bring Fadi, wrapped in his blanket, into this hospital, and I'd beg the American doctor to operate on him and bring him back to life. . . . And all the time I can hear Tzahi running around with the ball, and I can't stop picturing his brother with his rifle running around the alley.

My temperature has gone up again, and Vardina comes in and tells me that they're putting off the operation. Maybe it's my imagination, but her look seems to say that it's my fault.

It was the same in class when the teacher looked at me. I always felt guilty. It was me she looked at when Adnan, who sat beside me, smoked during the break. She always looked at me, never at Adnan. Even when I didn't take part in anything, I still felt guilty. There was always something to feel guilty about, especially with Adnan around. It's hard to be his friend without getting into trouble. Mom used to say to me, "The Blessed One gave Adnan's mother sons, but why do you have to be Adnan's best friend?" I get mad when she says this, but when I'm by myself I know she's right. With Adnan you're always doing things, and you never know how they'll end up. It always starts out promising and finishes with some trouble that hits you from nowhere. Sometimes I think that even if they gave Adnan a beating that would finish off a devil, he'd still be laughing.

That's how I am, lying here with a temperature,

torturing myself with bad thoughts. Every minute raises my chances of falling into the snake pit. But then something nice happened that made me forget for a few hours the postponed operation, the closed road-block, Tzahi's brother, and all the other troubles.

Fourteen

Ingrid One and Ingrid Two came and brought us some clay. The kind of clay that at home is used for making jars and pots, here they give to children to play with. Everyone got their own bowl with damp clay and a board to work on, and we can do what we like with it.

I sit for a long time, not daring to touch it. I watch to see what the others are making. Tzahi says he's planning to make a huge cannon. He needs a lot of clay, and he keeps running back to the cart to take more and more lumps. He kneads it with his huge hands, and he's so excited that the tip of his tongue is sticking out.

Yonatan is making a comet, but he has a problem with the tail. It's difficult to make a glowing comet tail out of clay. He sighs. While trying, he tells me about a comet called "Halley," which passes near the earth every seventy-six years.

A few years ago "Halley" passed nearby, and Yonatan's father took him out at night to see the comet. They went up a hillside, and halfway up Yonatan's father took him on his shoulders. Yonatan doesn't remember much more than that. He only remembers that it was cold and dark and the sky looked exactly like it always did at night. Some people were standing on the hill with Yonatan and his father, and suddenly someone shouted, "Look! Look!" and pointed at the sky directly overhead. But Yonatan didn't see anything other than the usual twinkling stars that he sees every night, even though he was sitting on his father's shoulders and was closer to the comet. Everyone got excited, included Yonatan's father. One old man started to dance on that dark hill in the middle of the night. Yonatan says that the old man was lucky that he got to see "Halley". It was the only opportunity of his life. When Yonatan is himself an old grandfather, perhaps he will get to see "Halley" the next time it comes around. Maybe he will also start dancing when he sees it, just like that old man.

Razia is trying to make a flowerpot for Vardina, in

place of the one broken by Tzahi's ball. But it's difficult to make a big pot. It keeps getting smaller and
smaller, until it's about the size of a saucer, but Razia
doesn't give up. She'd rather give Vardina a little
saucer than nothing at all.

Only Ludmilla lies back, doing nothing but looking at the window. She watches the flies buzzing on
the glass and dreams. Nothing that Ingrid and Ingrid
say, or the sentences I whisper — with or without
holding my breath — do anything for her.

I'd like to use the clay to make Fadi's rabbit, only I
don't know where to start — from the head or the
feet. Anyway, I still can't bring myself to touch this
damp stuff that sticks to the fingers. Whenever Fadi
and I played with mud, he would get it all over himself, clothes and everything, but I really hated to get
my hands dirty. Only when we made pretend falafel
balls out of mud, and dipped them in sand and put
them on a board, pretending to sell them — only then
could I forget about the mud for a while and get car-
ried away by the game.

Here in the hospital, they don't care at all if we
get dirty. Just the opposite. The more we get dirty and
smeared all over, the more Ingrid and Ingrid look happy.
It's all right to mess up the sheets and pillowcases,

because they'll be changing the bedding today anyway.

I take a big lump and start kneading it with my hands. The clay is cool and nice to touch. A lot softer than mud. You can smooth it and smooth it, and think about other things, and after a while your thoughts also get smoother and softer like velvet. You knead and you smooth, and soon you're no longer in this place. You're floating somewhere else.

This lump is still too big and shapeless for a rabbit; but there's plenty of time. I'm in no hurry. The rabbit is inside this lump: its four springy legs, the front two that hop and the back ones that bend and spring, and the tail. Even the head. Except that right now the body looks more like a sheep, rounded and plump, as if padded with soft wool all over. I start to pull the legs out of it, but no. They're too small and skinny, even for a rabbit. So now I've got a headless sheep with chicken legs. But there's no hurry. I know she's in there, and sooner or later I'll bring her out into the world. It's just a matter of time and patience.

Tzahi has already kneaded himself an enormous cannon barrel. It still doesn't have anything to rest on, this barrel, so he props it against the edge of his bowl, with the mouth pointing at the ceiling. Tzahi keeps making it longer and longer. He runs back and forth, fetching more lumps of clay.

I can't remember when I was so free to do what I want. Maybe in nursery school, but that was a long time ago. And there too I remember that it was always crowded and noisy. Too many kids stuffed into a little hut. Always pushing and yelling. Nobody had the patience to sit at a table and work at something. Anyway, the boys never sat down to draw or work at a table. They preferred to be out in the yard, playing wild games. In winter the roof leaked. It was never peaceful there, like it is here. Here we're just five kids with two teachers. So peaceful, you can hear the flies buzzing. Maybe that's how it is among the Jews. Maybe in their homes they live quiet lives, like the series on television. Sitting around sculpting in clay, eating rolls with sour cream and chocolate crispies.

I look at Yonatan, who's busy working on his comet, and suddenly I wish I was like him. I'd like it to be just Dad and me, and Dad would be mine alone. Maybe I'd miss Mom and Grandpa, but perhaps if Dad sat with me sometimes and talked to me, I wouldn't miss them so much. And at night, instead of sitting and sighing over the barbershop accounts, he would take me to look at the stars, just him and me.

Dad talks sometimes about the good days. How he and Mom got married a few months before the Occupation. About the thousand *dinars* they spent just on the sheep, the chickens, and sweet dishes, about the songs of Fairuz and the dancers, and the gladness of the guests, a real gladness that people don't even remember anymore. And in the kitchen Mom whispers about the women who rubbed her body with ginger, and the silk dress she wore, embroidered with golden swans, and the perfume that came from the dress. Then Grandpa gets mad at them for calling those days the good days.

There were other days — Grandpa grumbles — before the family was driven for the first time from its native city, when he was a boy. He describes the rooms of the house, cool and covered with carpets, and the room of his doctor father — which the kids could only peep into but were not allowed to enter — and the kitchen window that faced the blue sea, and the voice of the *muezzin* in the quiet nights. But then I see Dad shutting himself in a kind of silence, and I'm not so sure anymore that it all really happened. I don't know if I should believe Dad or Grandpa; if I should believe at all that life was ever so different.

I manage to fatten up the rabbit's legs, but they're still crooked and not at all nimble. It's not likely that anyone could hop on such legs. Maybe a goat — like the one on our neighbor's roof. That one doesn't hop much anyway. So now I have a sheep with goat's legs, and there's still a lot of work to be done. But I'm in no hurry. I think I'll tackle the head for a bit. The head can put a little life into this creature. That's right. I'm starting to bring the head out of the body.

Razia walks around the room, showing everybody her saucer and trying to figure out what it can be used for. Tzahi advises her to make little channels in the sides and turn it into an ashtray. Yonatan tells her that if she added a flat roof, it could easily turn into a flying saucer. But Razia is not sure Vardina would have any use for a flying saucer of this size. I'm not showing anybody my rabbit just yet. It's still far from being a rabbit. I pull a little lump out of the body and try to knead it on all sides. This will be the head. It's important to bring the head out of the body, not to add it from outside. After all, the whole rabbit is in there. I'm sure of that.

They even brought some special paints, those two Ingrids. The kind made especially for painting clay. Tzahi has already told us that he will paint his cannon in camouflage colors, to disguise it from the enemy. Yonatan is smiling to himself. He's thinking of making a nice little starfish. He crushes his comet and starts all over again. Ludmilla has turned around and lies with her face to the wall. She doesn't even want to see Ingrid and Ingrid.

Tzahi is running around with his cannon, shooting in all directions, and Yonatan is coloring his starfish with shiny silver paint.

You wouldn't say that it's a rabbit's head. It doesn't look a bit like Fadi's rabbit. It's too swollen, and the ears are too small. When I try to make them longer, they end up like two carrots stuck to the head. But when I draw her eyes she suddenly looks alive. She looks straight at me and doesn't look away. Those little ears actually suit her. No other ears would go with this look in the eyes.

Now this animal looks like an animal that couldn't exist, but it exists for me more than any other animal I know. The body of a sheep and the head of a summer cloud that looks straight at you. I give her a little tail, though I'm not sure she needs it. She's almost finished, and I sit and look at her closely. I wouldn't change anything about her. I think I won't even paint her. She looks more natural like this. Almost an earth color. Maybe just the eyes, then. In memory of the rabbit who died. I'll paint them purple — then she'll be ready.

All of a sudden, without any warning, Ludmilla's parents arrive. Two thin, smiling people, they come into the room carrying a cake with candles burning on it. They bring it in and sing a Russian song in high voices. It isn't just a party, Yonatan tells me. It's really Ludmilla's birthday. She herself forgot that it was today. Ludmilla sits up and stares at her parents and at the cake with wide-open eyes.

Ludmilla's father cuts her a slice of cake and — like in a fairy tale — Ludmilla opens her mouth wide and eats it from her father's hand.

Felix and Vardina come and clap. They take the tube out of Ludmilla's arm, and she sits with her parents and chats with them in Russian, as if she's never been sick in her life. Maybe the magic did help, after all. I don't know if it's from the times I held my breath, or the ordinary times. Or maybe it's just because I kept repeating those sentences as obstinately as a mule.

The children each give Ludmilla little presents. Tzahi gives her a handful of his American peanuts, and Yonatan gives her a peacock's feather. Razia gives her a bright rubber band for tying her hair, and I can only watch this celebration from my bed. But I tell myself that the magic was my present, and anyway, I'd be embarrassed to go and give a present to a girl who looks twelve, if not older. Felix starts to blow up balloons and hang them over Ludmilla's bed, and Vardina hands out slices of cake. We each get a piece of cake on a paper napkin.

I never saw such a cake in my life. It's not only covered with chocolate and snow-stuff on top of that, there are also tiny candies sprinkled on the snow. The cake itself is in several layers, each a different color. The white snow-stuff slips right into the throat before you know it. And the candies melt in the mouth. It's the kind of cake that you take one bite of, but then your teeth don't have anything more to do.

Ludmilla gets up and walks around the room with a piece of cake on a paper napkin in her little hand. She walks about, humming, and looking very happy. I love the sound of her white slippers with the silver embroidery. That's how it is with kids, I think. One moment everything looks black, the next moment everything's wonderful. It's like the saying, "One day honey, one day onion." Or as Adnan says, "Precious gold will always glitter, even in a heap of litter."

*   *   *

When they closed down our school, Adnan and I went to work collecting garbage. Sometimes everything was wet and stinky. It rained. The mornings were still dark. The guy who emptied the garbage cans into the truck shouted and yelled at us all the time to hurry up. We didn't even have time to peep into the cans before the truck came, and we had to run and drag out more and more cans and line them up beside the road. The air was freezing cold, and a kind of black grease stuck to our hands. It stuck and itched, and you knew that it would take hours to get rid of the smell. In the darkness, garbage is simply garbage, black and filthy. You know that nothing good will ever come from garbage. We rode and moved around in the poor neighborhoods. In all the garbage cans there was nothing but spoiled food, moldy beans, and burned falafel smelling of cheap frying oil that was used again and again. Torn plastic sandals. Worn clothes, falling apart. Adnan was wet and looked as if he was dunked in a barrel of tar, and even he wasn't laughing anymore.

But some days were different. The sun was bright. The rich people's streets were clean, and the driver moved slowly, like a tortoise, in no hurry to get anywhere. On those days Adnan and I had time to peer into the garbage cans. Adnan showed me how to shake out the can in such a way that it empties on one go. Then you look inside and see all kinds of colorful things. Sometimes they're just empty cartons or colored plastic bags, but you know, you just *know* that on such a day you're sure to find something.

Adnan said that once a boy found a box with six silver spoons in the garbage. Almost new, they were, he said. Just a bit worn at the tips. But with silver it doesn't matter. In fact, the more worn it is, the higher the value.

Sometimes, during those frozen black days, I thought it was just a story. A tale that grew in Adnan's head, the kind he came up with when he had nothing to do. Because sometimes he said they were spoons and other times little forks, the kind that rich people eat with. He himself didn't remember his own stories. But on good days, the warm days in the luxury neighborhoods, I was amazed to see what the Jews threw out. Perfectly good toys. Clothes washed and ironed, lying in a heap. Once Adnan found a leather hat with fur flaps that came down over his ears. The sticker from the shop was still in the hat! Somebody must have brought it from Russia and never even wore it. Adnan didn't take it off all winter. I once found a flashlight. It didn't work, but it was shiny red. I like flashlights. I don't care if they're broken. Even the tiny bulb, or the body of the flashlight without the insides. Adnan laughed at me. With a set of spoons you could buy a hundred flashlights. But I couldn't think about spoons. I looked like a hawk into the can and searched for flashlights, hoping I'd find one to pull out from the garbage before Adnan's eyes, like a magician pulling a rabbit out of a hat.

Ludmilla stops beside my bed and looks at the clay rabbit sitting on the board. I wish the earth would swallow me. I don't know what she's thinking. Right now the rabbit looks like a raw, shapeless lump. And with those stupid purple eyes that give you a queer look. I'm really sorry I painted those eyes. I'd like to hide under the blanket together with the rabbit. But Ludmilla smiles. I'm not sure, but it seems to me that she's seeing this animal just like I do. Otherwise, why would she smile? Yes, that's it. Maybe she can see in this animal the rabbit that is still inside but couldn't come out of the lump.

Ludmilla says, "May I?" She picks up the rabbit carefully with both hands and looks at it closely. As if it was a work of art. She pets it. I see Ludmilla's parents following every move she makes. They're smiling from a distance, but that doesn't mean anything, because they are smiling kind of people.

Without thinking, I say to her, "You take it," and pray that Tzahi doesn't hear. I really whispered, but Ludmilla heard. She walks away with the rabbit and lays it carefully on her bedside table.

There — one moment everything was black, and the next moment Ludmilla loves my rabbit. She loves it so much, she wants it near her, on her bedside table. So maybe I won't end up in Satan's snake pit after all.

Fifteen

In the morning I wake up hearing somebody weeping softly, and see Razia crouched under her bed, rolled up into a ball, her head on her knees.

Yonatan whispers to me that this time it's final. Her father is coming today, and her tears and cries won't stop him.

Vardina gets impatient. "He's your father!" she says again and again.

"I want Felix . . . ," wails Razia.

That only annoys Vardina more. "He's your father, Razia, and he has the right to come and see you."

So people lose patience here too, I say to myself. Not everything here is clay and chocolate crispies. I feel myself shrinking in my bed. I start being afraid, as on the first day. I just hope Vardina won't say anything to me. Won't talk to me in that tone of voice. That really hurts.

Everyone is getting restless. They didn't take our temperatures on time, and forgot to bring us rolls for breakfast. And I thought this place worked like paradise. I didn't know that Vardina could be so cranky. They come and talk to Razia. Draw the curtain, pull back the curtain. Razia comes out from under the bed, but she isn't looking any better. She sits on her bed, not saying a word. She looks like she's going to burst out again at any second. It's the scariest thing when you don't know what's going to happen in a moment. When you don't know what annoys people and what calms them down.

I remember the first time they searched our house. I was five years old, and Fadi was three. There were three of them. I can't remember their faces or the words they said. I only remember that they opened the cupboard where Mom kept the blankets, and Fadi crept in there, and sat down as if it was his house. Mom tried to pull him out of there and he screamed. The more she tried, the worse he screamed. His foot got stuck inside and he couldn't get it free. The more he twisted and turned, the more it got stuck. The soldier told Dad to get him out of there, but Dad couldn't free Fadi's foot. I could hear Fadi's screams, which deafened my ears, and see the soldier standing there with a rifle, but what frightened me even more was to see Mom and Dad looking like their wings had been cut, looking at each other, looking at Grandpa standing and banging his head against the wall. Fadi saw what was happening to them, and he took mothballs and threw them at Mom and Dad and Grandpa, all the time screaming with all his might.

Suddenly, Razia runs out into the corridor and everybody goes after her. First Tzahi, then Yonatan, and after a while Ludmilla too, in her embroidered slippers. I am left alone in the room. I hear people shouting in the corridor, footsteps running about, and a big uproar. Crying. Then silence. I sit quietly in my bed. The room looks strange when there aren't any other kids. A hospital room. That's how it looked the first day, when I was so confused I didn't notice everyone else. I begin to feel sorry for my parents. And for Grandpa and Bassam, if he's back from Kuwait. Even for Nawar. They're roadblocked in there, and I am here. They cling to the radio and television, but over there it's never clear what's going on. Sometimes you find out from neighbors. Sometimes from the bus driver. I don't know whether it's a curfew or something else. If they're stuck inside the houses and can't go to work, or if only traveling is forbidden and there are roadblocks everywhere. Maybe there's already a shortage of milk and bread. Maybe rumors are starting to go around, a different rumor every time, and people are rushing to buy food. Lines forming in the bakery, the grocery. Meanwhile I'm lying here having food brought to my bed. I feel ashamed to be lying here like the son of a pasha, as Grandpa would say.

Yonatan comes rushing in, pushing a wheelchair. He flies so fast that he crashes against my bed.

"Come," he says to me, and helps me to get out of bed and into the chair. I let him move me however he wants. I think that perhaps he's come to take me to Mars, but he wheels me to the end of the corridor. Tzahi and Ludmilla are waiting there for us.

Everybody's quiet. I see Tzahi looking more serious than ever. He speaks to us in whispers. He isn't looking at me, but I know he's speaking to me too. I don't know how it happened, but all of us kids from Room Six have become one group. It's all very serious now. Tzahi has a plan, which he tells us in a low voice, as if we are a company of soldiers moving under cover. As if all our lives have been directed to this purpose. Razia is hiding in the laundry room. The staff are all searching for her. Razia is in danger but we, a bunch of determined kids next to the elevator, won't let them find her.

"What can we do?" asks Ludmilla. Her eyelashes are long and fair, like the lashes of a princess. Tzahi silences her with a gesture of his hand. This is not the time for princess talk.

"So tell us," Yonatan urges him.

"We take up a position here beside the elevator, and when Razia's father shows up we don't let go. We stick to him like chewing gum, till he gets fed up to the teeth."

I can't believe that this is the kid who jumps up and down on his bed like a billy goat all day. He pushes his hand under his pajamas and tucks in the bag so it won't swing — like a fighter straightening his weapon under his coat. He looks only at Yonatan, as if he's the compass. Yonatan doesn't say a word, but his silence gives Tzahi strength. He never takes his eyes off Yonatan.

"How will we know that he's her father?" Ludmilla asks quietly.

She doesn't look like someone who could stick to a person like chewing gum. Right now she'd probably be happy to give up this whole adventure and go back to bed. But Tzahi isn't put off. He doesn't reply to her question.

"She and I will cover this elevator," he whispers to Yonatan.

As if the two of them had agreed that Ludmilla was Ludmilla and nothing could be changed now, so Tzahi volunteers to stand guard together with her. And then he says to Yonatan, speaking like he's used to giving orders: "You cover the staff elevator, in case he shows up at the end of the corridor."

"What about Samir?" Yonatan asks quickly, as if there's no time to lose.

"Take him with you!" Tzahi replies, still without looking at me. For a moment he resembles the pilot in that series about Americans at war. Talking into the mouthpiece, and looking ahead with cold, blue eyes.

Yonatan hurries to the other elevator, pushing me there in the wheelchair. As he runs down the corridor he keeps his head down, as if there's a jeep packed with soldiers chasing us. I hear shots in the air. Adnan is shouting to me, "Run! Run! Over the roofs!" and tears off ahead of me. I'm running, but my legs won't carry me anymore. It occurs to me that Fadi was also in the street, but I'm not sure. I think I saw him playing there. "Don't look back!" Adnan yells to me, then turns back and grabs me and forces me to come with him. I look back all the same — stop and look back. The alley is empty.

He didn't even look at me, that Tzahi. But I'm in the group now, we're all lion cubs together. Allah blessed our mothers and gave them male children. Life or death, with the good guys against the bad. For justice. For freedom.

The elevator goes up and down. Nurses, male and female, come and go. Beds on wheels come out of the elevator and go past. Yonatan sits on a bench and I in the wheelchair; we sit and watch the people. I try to picture Razia's father bursting out of the elevator, a bottle in his hand and a huge scar on his forehead.

Maybe an hour goes by. Vardina passes us in the corridor but doesn't speak to us. Doesn't even look at us. It's as if we're invisible. Felix has twice called us to come and eat our lunch. I'm thinking about Razia, crouched alone in the dark laundry room. I think about Fadi lying in the dark inside the earth, and he's a little baby.

I don't remember when he was born. I was too small. In my first memory he's about a year old or so.

I'm about three. Mom is changing his diaper on the low table. He's lying naked, moving his legs in the air. Also on the table there is a flowerpot with basil, and the smell of the plant mixes with the smell of the diaper. A patch of sunlight comes in through the window and moves on Fadi's face, and he moves his head and shuts his eyes, trying to escape from the patch. He's washed. His face is shiny and his curls soft as silk. He's new and fresh like a chick that's just hatched from the egg. Mom kisses him on his stomach and he laughs aloud. Always when I think about him there in the dark, he becomes again a washed baby, with a patch of sunlight on his face.

Then we see Tzahi and Ludmilla with a skinny man in a peaked cap. We see them through the glass door of the visitors' lounge, sitting and chatting with the man as if they know him. The man takes out a bag of apples and gives some to Tzahi and some to Ludmilla, and they accept. Tzahi and Ludmilla and the man eat apples and talk. Tzahi makes us a sign to come over. Yonatan goes first and I follow him, turning the wheels with my hands and advancing under my own power.

"This is Razia's father," Tzahi tells us, as if he's introducing us to the King of Jordan. "He's looking for Razia."

What about sticking to him like chewing gum? What about making him fed up to the teeth? I see that Yonatan is even more puzzled than I. He stands there with his mouth open, looking at the man, unable to say a word. To tell the truth, this man doesn't look a bit like what we thought. He's thin and a bit bent. He isn't holding a bottle and he doesn't look drunk. He has shaved and is wearing a clean shirt, and his hair is cut the same length all over his head. Somebody did a nice job on him, as my Dad would say. But above all, he looks at us with clear, smiling eyes, and there's nothing sneaky about them.

"Maybe you could go and call her?" Tzahi asks Yonatan politely, as if it's just an idea. Yonatan stares at Tzahi and at Razia's father and me, then again at Tzahi, but doesn't make a move.

"Then I'll go," Tzahi volunteers. "You guys wait here in the meantime."

And before anybody can say anything, he turns and runs toward the laundry room.

Razia's father takes out a bag of salted sunflower seeds and offers them to us. Ludmilla says, "No, thank you," but when Razia's father insists, she takes a few.

He then goes on to me and to Yonatan, patting us on the head and handing out seeds. And when Tzahi returns with Razia, he goes to her and hugs her as if he's meeting his lost daughter after years of suffering and hardship. He sits beside her, hugging and patting her, and can't calm down. Razia herself seems very happy. She looks at him — doesn't take her eyes off him — and never says a word. It's as if she has only been waiting for him to come, and I think how nice it is for her now to forgive him and get rid of all her anger. Now she has a new father, just for her.

We leave them sitting in the lounge and go away separately. By now there's no more group and no purpose and no courage, and Tzahi again doesn't say a word to me, either good or bad.

Sixteen

I mustn't think about Tzahi's brother. I must shake off this anger. If I want to have the operation before this doctor flies off back to Chicago, then I must stop thinking about Tzahi's brother and what he did to Fadi and all the rest of it, so my temperature will go down. But how can you make yourself stop thinking about something? Adnan says that if you think of the devil, the devil comes. The trouble is that even if you don't think about him, he comes anyway.

I used to think that I had to put up with Adnan and everything he said to me, even if sometimes he was more rotten than my shoes, because I'd never have a better friend than him. Even when he told me that I always ended up bringing him bad luck, I still put up with him and never complained. Now I'm not sure.

Every day Yonatan gives me his meatball or chicken or *schnitzel* or whatever they call it, and he never makes a big deal of it, and doesn't tell me seven times a day that I lack for nothing because I'm his friend.

One night Yonatan revealed to me that he and his dad never eat meat. He says it's not the fault of the cows and calves and the ducks and chickens that we like to eat them. He says that we — meaning people — have taken over the whole world and we keep destroying animals in huge numbers all the time. There are even some kinds of animals that are disappearing altogether; already there are only a few of them left, and it's a pity if any animal disappears, because, he says, it took us billions of years to get all these species in the world.

All the same, I don't understand how he thinks he's saving those animals by taking the meatballs from his plate and putting them on mine. But Yonatan says that if everybody did the same as him and his dad, animals wouldn't be killed anywhere. But I can put his mind to rest: The amount of meat we in the village eat is not what's going to finish off the animals. At this rate, I think they're perfectly safe and can go on living and developing, with their different species and all, just the way Yonatan and his dad want them to.

Here in the Jews' hospital I eat meat every day, and what I think will be hardest for me to give up is that canned minced beef that they give us on Saturdays. I once got to eat a lot of that kind of meat. It was when Adnan and I had a fabulous feast of army cans, after he came out of detention.

At that time, Adnan used to sell those cans of army beef in the market. He got them from Rafif, a woman who lived at the other end of the market, who got them from the Israeli soldiers who sometimes visited her at night. Rafif told him: For every ten cans you sell, you'll get one for yourself. Adnan went to the chicken seller and offered to pluck chickens for him all day, and in return the chicken seller would send him anyone who wanted canned beef. That's how he was going to sell them, one by one — but who was buying? Adnan plucked chickens for three days running, and only on the third day did someone come to him to buy a can of beef.

It so happened that I was passing by on the evening of the third day, when the soldiers showed up and started to search among the chickens and found Adnan's cans. So again he could say that I was the one who brought him bad luck.

Anyhow, they took Adnan into detention and

asked him a lot of questions and gave him a beating. But Adnan only said, "I got them from a woman on the street. I don't know her name; I don't know where she lives." And the way Adnan laughs in people's faces, it wouldn't have taken a lot for them to beat him to death. Except that his mother went and paid a thousand shekels and took him away. Adnan went home with his mother, and the cans were returned to the soldiers so they could go on visiting Rafif in the night.

Adnan went to Rafif and told her what happened, how the soldiers took away the cans, and of course he showed off and said he would have died and never let her name cross his lips. Rafif gave him tea and a coin, praising him and calling him a hero, and prophesied that with a heart of gold like his he would go far. But Adnan is no donkey or mule. Before he had ever even tried to sell the cans, he had buried three of them in the empty lot under the mulberry tree. Sort of keeping them in reserve. And so after he cursed me and said I brought him bad luck, we had a fabulous feast together behind the empty lot. That was in the days when Dad still allowed me to play outside after dark.

What finally brought my temperature down, I'm almost sure, happened one night, one of the nights when Yonatan and I stayed awake and looked at the stars. I was lying in a sweat, because of the pill Vardina gave me before bedtime to bring down my fever. I was hot one minute and cold the next. I'd pull the blanket up to my chin and shiver all over, and Yonatan said I was at the North Pole. Then I'd start sweating and kick off the blanket and open my pajama top, and then Yonatan said I'd reached the Sahara Desert.

And then he suddenly turned away from the window and came and sat on my bed, and said to me in that kind of seriousness that always amazes me: "Your trouble, Samir, is that you're always living in this world." He talks to me directly and simply, the way Adnan says to me, "Your trouble, Samir, is that you can't tell a goat turd from a Marlboro butt."

There is another world, Yonatan explains — never heard of such a thing in my life — and you can divide your life between this world and that other one. Nobody ever said that you have to pass your whole life only in this world, with everybody else. For example, if you run a fever you can simply slip away to the other world and live a good, healthy life there.

He's sitting on my bed, barefoot, playing with his thin braid, not even smiling or anything. But I already know that this boy is not the sort to pull a fast one, like Adnan. I've never heard him making up stories. Even though his stories about the stars sometimes sound like tales from *Thousand and One Nights*, he actually reads them out of serious books. And his father works in the business and he should know. But up to now, all the stories he's told belonged to our world. He never said a word about any other world. So I can't even think what questions to ask, I'm so amazed by this new discovery.

Say you've broken your knee, Yonatan goes on, and you're lying in bed like a lump. Or there's some problem with your arm and there are all sorts of things you can't do. Or maybe it's some other kind of trouble. Then you simply pick up and move to the other world, and nobody around you even notices. Because that other world — the grown-ups don't know about it. Even though some of them can see it, either they don't want to know about it, or they're so absorbed in this world that they can't feel the other one. This way, he goes on, you live right beside them, or they think that you're always right beside them, the whole time in this world of theirs, but you are not. You can slip away in no time to the other world and nobody even suspects. That is what gives you a kind of freeness, because in the other world you don't owe anybody anything. You don't have to explain or make excuses or tell lies or get in trouble. There you can do exactly what you want.

I look at this Yonatan and feel completely confused. I start to think that maybe there's something in what he says, something I never knew. I start to think that maybe all the time I saw him beside me, he really wasn't here at all. I start to notice little things I never saw before. I think about this quietness of his, and now he really seems to be from another world. I remember the long hours when nobody hears a sound from this boy at all. He lies in the bed next to mine, but he's not there. He says so little to me during the day, and so little to the other children. I say to myself that maybe during the day he isn't here at all; perhaps he only comes back at night. How can you tell?

"Maybe what you're talking about is a kind of dream," I reply, after a long silence. "You're wandering about in the other world, and it's all a dream. . . ." I'm trying to explain it to him, or maybe to myself. I don't know.

"A kind of dream . . . ," Yonatan repeats after me. He passes his hand over that yellow fuzz on his head. When he strokes it, it stays flat for a moment then springs back up, and again he looks like a slightly plucked chick. "Like a dream, but real. Not the kind you dream, but the kind that really exists."

"What do you see out there, in the other world?" I ask Yonatan. Now I understand him even less than I did before.

"Millions of things," he says, but doesn't explain.

"Tell me one thing," I insist. If Adnan was here, that's exactly what he'd be saying.

"Sometimes I see a girl who's looking for a key," Yonatan tells me. "She knocks on doors and meets all kinds of creatures who help her if they feel like it, or don't. She goes through dark forests, she sails on dangerous rivers, she encounters all kinds of animals, some scary and some sad. She needs power to fight the scary ones, and power can be got in a special shop, but she has to find the shop and that isn't easy. There are all kinds of ruses and obstacles. And in the shop, too, you must know what to choose. There's a handbook that explains it, but it's in a foreign language, and by the time you figure it out you're almost ready to give up. Because the shop has all kinds of power: There is the dragon sword and the giant's cudgel and the flying horse, which would give her speed, and the seven-league boots and —"

"And what do you do there?" I interrupt him, because now he's started to talk, he is making up for all the hours that he was silent.

"I help the girl," Yonatan says. "I go with her through the mazes and the caves and the forests, and try to figure out how to find the key that would take us to the airport from where we can fly to the green country, and all the time I hear a flute playing a sad melody, a melody without hope, which goes on as long as we don't find the key."

"Where does the music come from?" I ask, hoping Yonatan doesn't think I'm stupid. I still don't understand what he's talking about.

"From the computer," Yonatan says. "Where did you think it came from? But the music will change. In the end it will turn into music played by bells, as if somebody had hung bells on the trees in the forest and they swing in the soft breeze."

Then he moves closer to me, plants himself very near, looks me straight in the eye, and whispers: "Wait till my father brings me the software, then we'll be able to go there together, you and me."

I don't know what software is, and I'm ashamed to ask. But it doesn't make much difference. Now I'm sure that I'm the boy to whom Yonatan tells his most private secrets. Maybe there really is another world like that, and Yonatan will show me the way there. It's certainly nicer to think about than a pit full of snakes. I see him standing up on the bed, in the space between my feet and the end of the bed, looking out at the stars and humming for me the sad melody that the flute plays — the melody without hope that in the end, when he finds the key, will change into the music of a lot of bells of all sizes and shapes swinging in the soft breeze.

In the morning I wake up without a fever. I don't know if it's thanks to the flute music or the bells, or because Yonatan told me his secrets in such a calm, soothing voice.

Seventeen

In the hours leading up to the operation I was so woozy that I almost didn't feel any fear. Only in some lost little corner in the far end of my brain, a forgotten place, was fear still there, throbbing. Once again they take me on my bed through the corridors. I'm on the bed, but my head is flying above, the sort of feeling I had the first time I had a smoke with Adnan, behind the empty lot where in the past the young guys used to play soccer.

Trust Adnan to choose the mulberry tree behind the soccer field for us to sit in. The tree is where he wants me to sit when I smoke my first cigarette. It's not enough that I have to smoke, I also have to perch on a tree branch like a monkey. Never mind. Adnan cuts in half the Marlboro cigarette that he took from his uncle. He says his uncle gave it to him, but I know Adnan, don't I? Being Adnan, you can't even be sure he has an uncle. And if he has an uncle, does he even smoke? That's another question. And why would he suddenly give Adnan a cigarette, and a Marlboro too? Anyhow, Adnan cuts the cigarette in half and keeps the half with the filter. He even has a lighter. He doesn't say that he got the lighter from his uncle. He doesn't speak about the lighter at all. He lights his stub and breathes in the smoke with his eyes shut, like an old-time junkie. Only then does he light my half.

I breathe in a little smoke and blow it out quickly. Adnan is not pleased. Right away he shows me how to take it into the lungs. "If you don't inhale from the start," he tells me as if he's predicting my future, "you'll simply burn away cigarettes all your life." He sits and watches everything I do, like a teacher. I've got no choice. I take the smoke into my mouth and breathe it all the way in. A sharp knife goes down from my throat through all the tubes to the bottom of my stomach. I fight hard to hold back the cough that's trying to come up. My head flies off, but I'm still in the tree. I hold on to the branch and pray that the tree will stop swaying.

How I finished that cigarette I don't know, but I didn't dare give up. I kept on taking puffs, with longer and longer breaks, and blowing them out immediately. "Just filling the air with smoke," Adnan calls it. He has already finished his cigarette, crushed it on the sole of his shoe, and pitched it far away with two fingers, something I promise myself to practice when I'm by myself. Adnan sits watching me like I'm a prize donkey. "I don't know why I wasted my cigarette on you," he says, when we get off the tree at last.

I never went back to that tree with Adnan, but not on account of the cigarette. It was because Dad wouldn't let me go near the field after what happened there a few days before Ramadan.

Inside the operating room the ceiling is black and shiny, with dazzling lights beating on me from all kinds of lamps. Everybody's dressed in green clothes with masks on their faces, and I can't tell which one is the American doctor. I'm a little worried because I did want him, after he came all the way from Chicago, to be sure to do my operation. I know American doctors. I've never met any other kind, because it's the American ones I see every Monday evening in the television series after the news, whether there's a curfew or not. In fact, when there's a curfew they sort of help me to calm down.

Sometimes we know that they're going to blow up a house; then everybody stays home because we don't know when it will happen. Mom tries to get Grandpa to drink a glass of arrack, thinking it will make him go to sleep sooner, but he stubbornly sits and smokes, and the whole family knows what he'll do pretty soon when we hear the explosions and everything that follows. Dad is trying to paste up the big window, because it's already cracked and Allah knows what's holding it in place. He works with the sticky strips as quietly as he can, but Grandpa has the hearing of a wildcat. He doesn't miss anything that's going on in the room. He sits there, as alert as a fox. He even stops coughing at such times, just so he can hear better.

Sometimes in your own mind you wish they'd get on with it and finish. You stop thinking about the family and the kids that it's happening to, you just beg to be saved from the silence, which is worse than the biggest noise. . . .

And those people on the television screen keep going around in their green clothes and wide smiles,

and the cleverest women doctors — who are for-
tunately always good-looking. Even if there's a lot
of pressure and tons of work to do, they still have
enough time to smile and worry about some lonely old
woman, or about a cowboy who's incredibly brave
but scared of operations, even though he doesn't
admit it. And you wonder how the top doctor who's
like a father to everybody always knows how to give
the right advice here and extra respect there, and a
nice pat for that patient, and it makes you feel good
thinking that there are such people in the world. . . .

Now one of the green people takes off my pajamas
and dresses me in a long white shirt that ties in the
back. I'm so woozy I don't mind. I feel like a baby that
has everything done for him and doesn't need to
worry about anything, only smile at the people who
are so pleased with him. I'm lucky that Tzahi can't see
me in this dress.

"In a moment you'll be sound asleep, Samir," one of
the green ones says. "And when you wake up, it will
be after the operation." She gives me an injection, and
she must have the hands of a fairy, because I don't feel
anything. On the contrary, the injection must have
made my heart bigger, so my blood warms up and

flows peacefully like it should, and I can see the doctor's eyes above me, smiling at me. That's him, I'm sure it's him. It even seems to me that he's chewing gum under the mask. Now I'm perfectly relaxed.

"Start counting," a woman doctor says to me gently — or is she a nurse? They all look alike, like the children of the same mother. And they're all here for me, surrounding the bed and looking at me, not doing anything else. I start counting. The Arabic numbers sound peculiar in this room. In this place the numbers are mine only, nothing to do with anybody else in this room. Pity that in English I can only count to nine. If I could count in English, I'd get into the television series and become part of it. I'll never know what number I reached. Between numbers I'm swinging with this bed, feeling more and more peaceful. I also remember thinking: What happens if I don't wake up? And another crumb of a thought: If I die, maybe my family will steal me from the hospital, like they stole Fadi, although nobody ever explained to me why. It stuck in my mind and sometimes it bothers me, like all the things you don't understand and you put aside, thinking that maybe one day you will understand them. But you can't even be sure of that.

There are too many things nobody understands.

It's not just a question of your age. You know that. Your dad and grandpa are no better at it than you. My grandpa says: "There's too much confusion in the world. A simple man, even a cunning one, can't imagine the truth behind the stories they tell." Just as nobody can say exactly who shot Ali, our neighbors' son, just after he kicked the ball into the goal on the soccer field. Just when he was jumping for joy, right after the goal, and his buddies were running over to hug him, somebody aimed a gun and shot him. You never know anymore where the bullet will find you. Grandpa says you could be waiting for the soccer ball to come your way, and get a bullet instead. And you don't know if it's the soldiers, or the avengers, or soldiers pretending to be Arabs. I'm lying on the bed in the middle of this confusion, and the confusion gets heavier and heavier and starts to drag me down. I dive deeper, very slowly, and disappear from this room together with the bed to a quiet, faraway place. . . .

Eighteen

Maybe it was the anesthetic that made me dream such a long-long dream as I never dreamed before. Usually when you sleep at night and you finish a dream, you turn over to the other side and start the next dream, or else wake up for a moment, lie quietly, and rest. But here you can't turn over and can't wake up until the anesthetic finishes, so you go on and on with the dream, and you have no choice, even if you don't have the strength to dream. You have to go on. So it happened that I spent the whole time of the anesthetic wandering with my grandpa on a long trip that refused to end, on paths that I didn't know, in villages and cities that I never saw, in a kingdom that Grandpa called the kingdom of Samarkand. . . .

We walk in villages, marching along blue rivers with light boats sailing on them; we climb snowy mountains, and wash our bodies in the water that rushes down in the waterfalls. From there we go on to a white city on the seashore, and walk through the streets, looking at the shops that are full of all the good things of the land, and gardens hanging over springs of fresh water in the middle of the city, and markets with wonderful fruits and vegetables that we never saw before. Nobody greets us, and we don't know any of the local people. Then, on the corner of a street that overlooks the port, we sit down on a bench beside a tower with a big clock, and Grandpa tells me that he was once a king.

I look at Grandpa and he's not dressed at all like a king. His clothes are old and torn. Alarmed, I look at my own clothes, and see that they're also shabby and ragged, like Grandpa's clothes. I wonder how I never noticed it before now. Evening is coming, and I'm very tired from our journey, and hungry and thirsty too. I ask Grandpa where we're going to eat, where we're going to drink, where we're going to rest — but he doesn't answer. I ask Grandpa if he knows anybody in this country, someone who would let us rest under his roof, but Grandpa doesn't know a soul here. I think to myself, how is it possible that he used to be king in a place where he doesn't know a single soul? But I don't dare ask him. I wait. I hope that we shall be saved in some way. We continue walking and walking, but again don't seem to get anywhere.

I look at Grandpa and see that his face is full of sadness. More than tired and hungry, he looks like a man weighed down with a great sorrow. He is so sad that he can't take care of the tiredness or hunger anymore. Sad and defeated, he walks ahead of me and never once looks into my eyes.

We reach the city square, a wide space in front of the palace. The palace is built of white stone, and has lots of minarets and towers. Flags fly from the towers and a band plays the national anthem. The royal guards stand armed to protect the palace gate and make sure no stranger can enter. Then, all of a sudden, the street is in an uproar: One of the guards who had been carrying the princess's litter stumbled and fell, almost dropped the princess, and now they're calling for a young man to come out of the crowd and take the guard's place.

I suggest to Grandpa that I should try my luck and help them carry the princess, and maybe they'd give me a coin. Grandpa gets mad at my ignorance and naughtiness. It's unthinkable that someone of our family, the royal family, should work as a porter for other people, he declares. What a shame and a disgrace that would be! But I plead with him in the softest words. Work has never shamed anybody. And after all, it's not like we're begging. At last he gives in. We have no choice. If we don't do something, we'll perish of hunger and thirst. Very unwillingly, he lets me go. I join the guards, pick up the corner of the litter, and walk with them as we carry the princess into the palace.

The inside of the palace is filled with a brilliant light. I watch as the princess steps slowly out of the litter, walks to her throne, and seats herself on it. Suddenly, I notice her white cloth slippers embroidered with silver thread. For a moment I can't remember where I saw them before, but when I look closely at her face I discover that she is Ludmilla.

Princess Ludmilla claps her hands to tell the guardsmen to leave her alone with her maids, and I'm at a loss. I know that if I leave this room and go out with just a coin in my hand, it would be as if I left empty-handed. Grandpa is waiting outside, and even more than his hunger, it is the despair in his eyes that hurts me now. I decide to risk it and stay in the room. I must speak to the princess, whatever the cost. I beg her forgiveness and beg her to let me speak to her in private and tell her my story. She says nothing, but looks at me questioningly, so I start talking quickly. I tell her in a few words about the troubles we've been through — the hunger and the thirst.

The princess listens intently to my story and reassures me. She herself has not eaten or drunk anything in many days, she says — but she does not tell me the reason why. Nothing is easier, though, than to tell her servants to feed me and my grandfather, she explains. Once again, I feel at a loss. I must tell her the whole truth. Must tell her that we are strangers in this country: about my grandfather's great sadness, and how once, in the past, he was the king.

Only I myself doubt it. When I look at my grandfather he doesn't look like someone who was once a king. He looks much more like a market porter. His face is weather-beaten, and he's all shriveled from smoking cigarettes. I'm afraid the princess will laugh at me if I tell her a story that sounds made up.

She sits on her throne, looking at me. She sees that something is troubling me but doesn't know what it is. She urges me to tell her what is in my heart.

I tell the princess about the deep sorrow in my grandfather's eyes, and hint at the better days he had known, though I don't dare speak about the lost kingdom. But the princess seems to understand much more than what I reveal. She orders the servants to provide me with food and drink, and also gives me a present for Grandpa: a small prayer rug trimmed with beads. I thank her for the beautiful gift, but decline to take anything from her. I know that the prayer rug, no matter how beautiful and appealing, will not erase the sorrow in my grandfather's eyes.

But the princess laughs like a tinkling bell and explains that this is not an ordinary prayer rug, but a magic carpet that can carry whoever sits on it anywhere at all — even to the planet Mars. "If your grandfather flies with you," she says, "he will return to better times." I am very moved by her words. I thank her, and she bids me farewell.

Grandpa and I sit down on the rug and we fly over the king-dom. For a little while the sorrow leaves Grandpa's eyes. He hugs me while we float over fields and meadows. I would be happy to sit on the rug forever and look at him. I can hardly believe my eyes: My grandfather is laughing! But after we have flown and glided about all day, I see the sorrow gradually returning to his face.

We land, and once more we are strangers dressed in rags, once more hungry and thirsty. The magic carpet vanishes, and despair once again settles in Grandpa's eyes.

I decide to go back and find the royal palace. Maybe I'll be able to go in and ask the princess for another gift for my grandfather, and maybe that gift will really make him happy, and he will forget that sorrow of his forever. But we have traveled over cities and villages, and nobody has heard of the land of Samarkand. We have arrived in the land of Bishangra.

Again, we don't know a living soul in the land of Bishangra. Once more we wander, hungry and thirsty, in markets full of all good things. And once more we have no roof over our heads. And now, in one of the city streets where the sidewalks are trimmed with precious stones, a town crier announces that the princess, the king's daughter, has fallen gravely ill. To whomever succeeds in curing her, the king will give a wonderful gift. I join the line of young men and boys who wish to enter the palace. It's a long, weary line. I stand there for seven days and seven nights, awaiting my turn. A hundred young men have already tried their best, but none has succeeded in curing the princess.

They lead me into a room filled with bright bluish light, in the middle of which lies a big bed decorated with silvery olive leaves and hung with pomegranates. The princess is lying full-length on the bed, pale as the full moon, with a tube that the doctors have stuck into her arm. I approach the bed and see that she looks exactly like Ludmilla — only her hair is dark, not gold.

At once I command them to prepare a birthday party for the princess. I summon her parents and order them to come in with a chocolate cake covered with snow-stuff and candies, and all kinds of presents. At first the king is annoyed with me for treating his daughter's illness so lightly, for not understanding how serious it is. But when he and his wife enter with the cake (and I insist that they come in singing and smiling), and see the princess sit up, take the tube out of her arm, and begin to devour the chocolate cake, the king and queen fall on my neck and give me gifts and send me on my way with great honor and ceremony.

My grandfather waits for me at the palace gate all those days. His body has shrunk and dried from hunger, and the clothes he's been wearing have become even more ragged. The despair in his eyes is deeper than ever. He does not care about the presents I have brought. Only one gift, a rare and special one, attracts his attention. It is an ivory pipe with a lens at the end. When you look through it, you can see the good old days. When my grandfather looks through the glass he begins to smile, and then to laugh. He hugs me and chuckles, and then cries for joy. Then he shows me the sights that can be seen through the lens. I see a flock of goats grazing on a hillside, and a barefoot shepherd with a staff and knapsack sitting down in the shadow of an ancient olive tree, calmly eating a chunk of cheese dipped in olive oil. But I don't see any palaces or precious stones, and once again begin to doubt Grandpa's stories. I am ashamed of my disbelief and put my hand in Grandpa's hand, and we set out again to look for his lost kingdom.

We wander on foot, along wadis and across rivers, until finally we reach the city of Shiraz.

The streets of Shiraz are empty. The inhabitants have shut themselves in their homes and the gates are locked. No one can come in or go out. We walk through the silent marketplaces and the empty squares, never seeing a single human being. Only a wind blows the dry leaves, and a lame hen hobbles in the middle of the road.

We continue walking down all the streets of the empty city, till we reach the building of the Administration. It is surrounded with barbed wire, and the gate is shut. Beside the gate sits a guard, blowing up balloons and letting them fly away, because he has nothing else to do. I ask him when the next break in the curfew will be, and he smiles at my innocence and says, "All the breaks have been canceled." I beg him to take me before the king's daughter, and he gives me a strange look and mutters, "I'll take you to the woman-officer, if you insist." We go into the Administration building. The corridors are full of people standing in long lines, waiting. The guard takes me to a far room with bare walls. There, behind the desk, sits a woman-officer. She looks like Ludmilla, only her hair is black as tar. I peer down to see whether she's wearing the white slippers with silver embroidery, but the room is so dark I can't see them.

The officer looks at me and I feel ashamed to be standing there in my ragged clothes. She asks me, "Have you taken a shower? Did you scrub behind your ears?" I swallow the insult and wait a little before telling her about my tired and hungry grandfather, who is waiting outside. Then I begin to speak. I want to tell her about the past of my father and grandfather and where they came from, about the good lands and the grazing goats, about the shepherd and the ancient olive trees. By this time, I myself don't believe in it as much as before. I find it difficult to imagine what used to be. She sees this in my eyes, and she interrupts me and says dryly: "I have no more gifts. A person who doesn't believe that his grandfather is a king will always be a market porter for strangers." Then she sends me out of the building.

I go outside, ashamed and in despair, and see that Grandpa is gone. I run through the empty streets, searching for him, calling him by name, but the streets are quiet. Silence. There are no human voices. I look up, far toward the hills, and see Grandpa. He's standing on the edge of the desert. I call to him, but he does not turn around. He starts to walk into the desert. I want to run, but my legs won't move, and one leg is stuck to the ground. . . .

Nineteen

I wake up lying in a big room full of beds. I make an effort and manage to twitch my toes a bit, but my legs are like rocks, as if they've never moved. My knee hurts. I'm so woozy that for a few moments I forget who I am and where and why I'm in this place, and think that my knee is hurting from that long journey in the dream. The man in the bed on the right is moaning aloud. On my left, there's a woman who looks as white as her sheet. A girl is giving her a few drops of water on a stick with wet cotton that she lets the woman suck. A nurse goes to the moaning man and speaks to him in a low voice. I'm the only one alone.

My whole body hurts, but my head most of all. Two hammers are pounding on the sides of my head, keeping beat with my pulse. I call out, "Yamma,

Yamma . . ." I know Mom isn't here, but I've got to call out to her. I feel that I'm shouting, but my voice comes out so weak, it can hardly be heard. If I don't yell out loud, I'll faint and they'll forget me here.

Then I doze for a few minutes and the pains take a little pity on me. I open my eyes again a bit later. Just keeping them open is an effort. In my short naps I see quiet pictures. Blue lakes, like those on the doctor's wall from the first day. I throw a stone and make it skip a few times on the surface, the way Adnan did once on the big rain puddles in our village. This time I succeed. I remember what Adnan and I talked about beside the biggest puddle.

"I've never seen the sea," I said to Adnan.

"So what?" Adnan said.

"If we lived in the Gaza Strip, at least we'd be near the sea," I said.

"I have uncles living in the Strip," Adnan said, "but you can be sure their kids have never seen the sea."

I'm not even sure he has uncles in Gaza. Adnan has relatives where it's useful, that's for sure.

"Anyway, what do you need the sea for?" Adnan asked. "That's what's missing in your life? Just pretend there's no such thing as the sea, all right? What's the sea, anyway?"

I couldn't explain to Adnan what the sea is. I myself don't know what it is.

"Anyway, you can't swim," he went on. "You'd go in and drown."

How can I know how to swim if I've never been to the sea? If I've never even seen the sea from a distance? "In my mind I know what I miss," I told him. "I'm missing something big, something that doesn't have a fence or a roadblock in front. Something that belongs to everybody. To God, maybe."

"The cinema in the town," Adnan said after a long silence, "the one they just closed down — it belonged to my cousin." He started making up new cousins.

"No honestly," Adnan swore by all that was sacred to him. "Ask anyone you like. It was my cousin's cinema, it was. They took me there once when I was little. I slept through the whole movie. There were kids selling roasted beans in the breaks. My dad went out to smoke in the hallway. I went out with him and he bought me roasted beans and we looked at pictures from the movies. It was the most wonderful evening of the time when I was small. Now my cousin has closed down the cinema. It was the last one that was still open in town, but nobody came to see the movies. Nobody goes out in the evenings."

"What's that got to do with the sea?" I asked him.

We were sitting together in the dark beside the big puddle. We had nowhere to go, we had nothing to do. We talked about the sea and the cinema, but we didn't really believe there was a world outside the darkened village. Once we used to sit there and look at the lights of the town. We dreamed about what we would do when we grew up and went there. A stray dog passed nearby. Adnan threw a stone in its direction and the dog ran away, yelping. The yelp got on my nerves. "What's that got to do with the sea?" I asked again. Quarrel with Adnan, that's all that was left for me that evening.

I go back to my blue lake, throw stones, and make them skip three, four, five times on the water. Too bad Adnan isn't in my dreams. Too bad he can't see me making the stones skip.

They wheel away the bed of the woman on my left and put an empty bed in its place. The man on my right was taken away when I slept. Why don't they take me away? Why did they forget me in this place? There's no air here, I say to myself. I must return to the lake. At least there I could breathe a little. But now I can't fall asleep anymore. I'm wide awake. I feel a little like I did the first day in the Jews' hospital —

as if somebody stuffed a big stone in my belly. Again I try to move my toes. They feel as cold as ice. I get scared and yell. A nurse comes over, checks all the gadgets, and wets my lips a little.

"They'll soon come to fetch you," she says.

"My hands are cold," I say.

"Why are you afraid?" she says. "You're not going to die." She laughs and walks away, her sandals slapping on the floor.

Sometimes I get a peculiar idea. Instead of my brother Fadi, it's me who's wrapped in a big blanket and laid on the table at home. Not a very big package, a pretty skinny one. With a big bloodstain at the end. I'm lying there without moving. Mom is looking at me with unseeing eyes, like Grandpa's. My sister Nawar is crying. Grandpa says we must tell Bassam, but nobody hears him. Dad's standing right beside me, and his mustache trembles. A neighbor comes in and tells them something about a shot. The bullet struck my back. When they brought me to the hospital I was still alive, but the bullet made a hole in a lung. I was no longer conscious. . . . Dad hugs me, blanket and all. He squeezes me tight and forgives me for everything. From now on, he whispers, he won't let anyone separate us, ever.

This moment with Dad, I have to go back to it all the time. The moment when Dad hugs me tight and I'm almost happy to have a hole in my back. There's only me and Dad in the room. If I could weep I would, but I'm dead. Still, I feel Dad's arms around me the whole time. Even dead people can feel such a thing.

All of a sudden a nurse bends over me and says in pure Arabic: "Where are you from, boy?"

I'm still a bit woozy. I raise myself a little and answer, "I'm from Jaffa."

"I'm from Jaffa too," she smiles at me, showing white teeth. Then she looks at the sheet of paper hanging on the end of my bed. "Aren't you the boy from the West Bank?" she says.

"My grandfather was born and grew up in Jaffa," I tell her in Hebrew. "His father was a big doctor over there." I'm trying to speak out loud. I want everyone in the recovery room to hear me.

She examines my knee and goes on in Arabic: "And where is he now, your grandfather?"

"They had a big house," I go on in Hebrew. She smooths my pillow and I raise my head as far as I can, so they'll all hear me. "The house faced the sea."

She asks in Arabic, "Was it a nice house?"

But I persist in speaking Hebrew. I want everybody to hear Grandpa's story. "It was a beautiful house," I tell her, "with lots of rooms and many windows and plenty of air."

Finally she understands my game. "And what is there today, in your grandfather's house?" she asks in Hebrew. She laughs shyly. She's not used to speaking up.

"A café," I reply, and laugh aloud and she laughs too. She laughs at my laughter, at the game we're playing which we both understand. She covers her mouth with her hand to stop laughing, but she can't. She looks as if it's been a long time since she laughed aloud in this place, and it's bursting out of her. She can't stop the laughter that's trying to make up for all the time that she didn't laugh. We are very loud, but the patients seem too sleepy to care, and those who aren't sleepy are thinking about their pains. I don't believe anybody here even hears us and our big laugh.

Twenty

Going back to Room Six was almost like going home. I heard Razia's voice shouting: "Here he comes! Here he comes!" And all the kids ran into the room to see what I'd do when I saw the balloons they'd hung over the bed and the candy they'd hidden under my blanket. The first thing I do is look at Ludmilla's bed. Her hair is again the color of gold. She is sitting and looking at me without saying a word, but we both know what we went through together, and there is no need to speak.

I thought that they'd bring me all the meals I'd missed, but that's not how it's done. They brought me a light meal, and I had to wait a few hours for that too.

"The stomach has to gradually get used to food

again," Vardina explained to me, then went to sing to her plants.

I sat up and wolfed down the whole little meal. I thought I could swallow a mountain. It was hard not to stuff myself quickly, but Felix came and sat beside me and kept slowing me down: "Easy, easy now!" As if I was a little baby who still doesn't know how to eat.

I surprised myself by eating some kind of white stuff with much pleasure. It was in a cup like sour cream, but didn't have the good taste of it. I swallowed it as if it was another birthday cake of the Jews.

The kids sat and watched me eating. Yonatan sat there also and didn't take his eyes off me, even though food is the last thing in the world that he cares about. It was very quiet as they sat and watched every spoonful I put in my mouth, as if it was the act of a hero. Honestly, I was sorry to finish this meal. I'd have liked it to go on and on.

But something had changed in the room. At first I couldn't figure out what it was. It wasn't just that Tzahi wasn't running wild with the ball, or jumping like a billy goat, or leaping like a paratrooper from bed to bed. It was something else. For the first time I noticed his eyes — they stopped moving all the time and now looked straight ahead. He was sitting quietly on the bed, looking at me, and so I noticed his eyes. But I said to myself, Don't start celebrating, Samir. Under this look, who knows if this sly type isn't cursing the bones of your ancestors in his heart.

They brought me a telephone without a wire to the bed and said that Mom was on the line. I could hardly hold onto the receiver, which had a lot of buttons on it. Any other time I'm sure I'd have liked to play with those buttons, but now I didn't even think of pressing them, because suddenly all the weakness from the operation came down on me. I told Mom everything was all right, but my voice was weak and Mom kept repeating that she couldn't hear me. As if I wasn't used to speaking Arabic anymore. I asked if she managed to get flour and sugar for the curfew, and she laughed and said, Is that what's worrying you now? In the end I wanted to ask if Grandpa was back from the desert, but stopped myself in time and shut my mouth.

Only in the night do I hear from Yonatan. He didn't open his mouth until the sun went down. Only when darkness filled the windows, then he began to wander about the room restlessly. I hope he wasn't planning to go on the journey tonight, because I don't have the strength to move. Yonatan waited for everyone to go to sleep. But it wasn't easy. They were all so excited today that it was difficult to get them into their beds. Felix came with his flashlight to see whether everyone was in bed, but they moved about and giggled, and Yonatan got into bed and covered himself and breathed deeply. Maybe he thought it would influence the others, but it didn't. Felix didn't get mad. He just said he'd be back in a little while, and hoped to find everybody off to the Land of Nod. I thought then that if they sent somebody like him to guard the men in prison, maybe it wouldn't be so bad in there.

At last when everybody was asleep, Yonatan comes and sits on my bed and reads me the poem he wrote about our planet:

> Four billion years —
> just seaweeds.
> Four billion years —
> Just marshes.
>
> Nothing but water everywhere —
> Ho ho ho,
> the planet's sleeping.

Half a billion years more —
Here is life:
Fishes, lizards,
Plants, and storks.

Just a few million more —
oh clever planet!
Ho ho ho! —

Man arrives at last!

He finishes reading it, folds the paper, and puts it under my pillow. Then I understand that the poem is for me. Maybe I should clap my hands. But I don't want to wake the sleepers, and Yonatan is already climbing up to the window to watch the stars, as he does every night.

Suddenly he says to me without turning his head: "I kept a meatball and a chicken wing for you, but Vardina didn't let me keep them in the drawer. She took them out and threw them away." I start to laugh, picturing Vardina opening the drawer and finding the pieces of meat in there. . . . But also because I understand that while I was over there in the operation, and all the time I was under the anesthetic, Yonatan never forgot me, even if he spent the whole time in that world of his, where he moves around with such freeness.

Yonatan already knows what is to come. You think that once the operation is over you're all done and can go home, but it isn't so. They're in no hurry to let you go, he says. That's exactly what Bassam told me happened to him in prison, when we needed all the lawyers that Mom cleans for to make the prison give him up.

After the operation they'll take you into rehabilitation, Yonatan explains. That's to accustom your arm or leg or knee or whatever to do everything it used to do naturally before. And if you can't walk, you get a wheelchair, so one of these nights soon we'll be able to make the journey to the planet Mars.

The next few days after the operation I don't ask him much about it, because I am still too weak from the anesthetic to think about going to space, and in a wheelchair too. In the meantime the only trip I take in the wheelchair is with Felix, but it's only to the rehabilitation ward where I go every morning and stay till lunchtime.

At first I was supposed to try to walk between two iron bars — and I couldn't believe it! Before the operation I could still step on the leg with the broken knee, but now even touching the floor with my foot while holding onto the bars with both hands gives me such pain that I want to scream. It feels like they didn't fix my knee, only made it worse. But Felix promises me that tomorrow it will be a bit easier, if only I do exactly what he tells me to do.

The next morning he asks me if it hurts less. It hurts just as much, but I don't want to disappoint Felix, so I say it's a little better, so he won't despair. In my heart I say: Forget about soccer. If you can limp half as fast as the lame sahlab seller, say thanks to Allah and don't ask for more.

I do everything in the rehabilitation ward just to please Felix. It's tricky. He promised me so seriously that everything will be all right soon, that I don't like to prove him wrong. I make all this effort between the two rails, and in the end I see that Felix is sweating more than me. And after all the exercises, when we're both exhausted, he helps me lie on my stomach on a mattress and starts to take care of my back. Because the back, he says, is our weakest part.

Out of all the animals, only humans got up on our hind legs and insisted on walking upright, in spite of all the problems. But the problems knock us down flat. And if you lie down a long time, your back becomes useless. So every day Felix takes off his ring and pours some oil into his hands and rubs them together, then he starts to walk them on my back, round and round. I just lie on my face doing nothing. If Grandpa could see me, he would scold me and tell me to get up on my two feet right away, because I'm behaving like the spoiled son of a pasha.

One day I looked at Felix's ring, which he took off so he could move all over my back more easily, and I noticed that it's exactly the same as the ring that Dad wears on his little finger. This one is also engraved with a palm and a mountain, and on the mountain, right on the horizon, a camel walks toward the sun. Only Dad's ring is green and Felix's is dark brown.

All of a sudden, while lying on my stomach with nothing to do, letting Felix travel his fingers over my back, I start to play the game of "transfers."

"Transfers" is a game that Adnan and I sometimes used to play in the evening when we had nothing to do, when there was still soccer and a few teams were still playing, until that too was stopped. It's a good game to play in the evening in the village, like when there's curfew, or any evening when Dad locks and bars the door and doesn't let me go outside, so I can only play with my neighbor Adnan through the hole in the bathroom wall. Then it doesn't matter if there's an electricity cutoff or a water cutoff or any kind of cutoff they can think of.

It goes like this: Each person adopts a soccer team and can transfer players from other teams into it. Most of the game is about these transfers, and there's a lot of arguing and arbitration and haggling, because each side wants to have the best players, and the one who has the most patience and can talk fastest and get ahead of the other finishes up with the first-rate team. Then, when you've agreed on the compositions and stopped arguing, you can start to play. It's all talk. You've got to keep the field in your mind, also the new players that you've moved, and of course the ball, so you can describe the passes and the goals and the fouls and everything. All from your head.

The darkness in the bathroom helps to keep the picture clear in your mind. You don't even have to close your eyes. You can't see anything anyway, only the soccer field. If you goof, or say something that can't happen, the ball passes to the other team. Then your partner starts to describe how his team is breaking into your team's goal.

We called this game "transfers," because the part we like best was building up the teams and transferring players from other teams to ours. If you do it well, all your games will be better.

So now in the rehabilitation ward, I play the game with myself. I don't know how the idea came to me — perhaps because Felix's ring is the twin of my dad's ring. I play at transferring Felix to be my dad, and my dad to be Felix.

First I move Felix to our house, and at night he comes to my bed with the flashlight to check if I'm off to the Land of Nod. But that isn't special. That's exactly what he does here in the hospital. I want to see how very slowly the exchange will begin to change their two lives. I transfer Dad to the hospital, and here he looks after patients, pulls balloons out of their ears and blows them up, while Felix in the village gets up at dawn every morning and opens the barbershop, where nobody comes to get a haircut. Felix doesn't know what to do with his energy. He hangs up a sign saying he will treat your back for the price of a haircut. But people don't have time to think about their backs, and anyway they don't have any money, and a man who needs a haircut gets his mother to give him a trim, or his wife, or his sister. So Felix gets a bit bored. He's not the sort who likes to sit around doing nothing.

Then I think that Dad could really be in Felix's place, not just in a game, and Felix could be in Dad's place, and there wouldn't be anything funny about it. It would all look the same, only the other way around. Dad would be here, looking after the sick children and caring about them, and wouldn't think even once a day that Felix is stuck out there in his house because of the curfew. Maybe he wouldn't even know what curfew means. It wouldn't be in his mind. I can see Dad walking down the corridor, rolling a heavy bed into the elevator, and it looks perfectly normal.

Then I see Felix standing beside our house, seeing men coming and fencing off our orchard of olive trees, so that it isn't ours anymore. Felix goes up to the man who is doing this and the man says to him: "*Rookh min hone!*" — "Go away!" Then I try to imagine that the man saying "Rookh min hone" is my dad, but that's a lot harder. I force myself to put my dad into the body of the man who's fencing our trees with barbed wire, because that's the game. But I can't picture the man's face, and I'm not sure that the transfer's working. But I insist, and in the end I hear the man saying "Rookh min hone" to Felix and his voice is my dad's voice. . . .

Felix can't understand why my dad is talking to him like this, and asks why they're taking away his olive trees. Now my dad says these words with a Jews' accent, then turns his back on Felix and goes away.

Later I transfer Tzahi and Yonatan to our alley, and I move into Yonatan's house. Tzahi's doing pretty well out there, with Adnan and the boys. He runs with them through the smoke and escapes from the bullets; he doesn't stick out too much over there. Meanwhile, I go with Yonatan's father to see the stars at night. Only Yonatan doesn't fit in one bit in our alley. No, I have to bring him back. It's just not for him.

And all this time Felix is moving his hands all over my back, which is still sore from lying on it all these days. I think how much work must be put into a back so that it will be straight and not hurt — but still, how you can shoot a rifle bullet into such a back and finish it off, together with the person, in two seconds flat. So now I play "transfers" with Fadi and me: It could so easily be Fadi lying here now, with Felix working on his back. And me — it could easily be me lying in the ground over there.

At night Yonatan tells me about what happened to Tzahi, why all of a sudden he's lost his fire like a candle. In a few days the doctors are going to take away the tube and bag, but they have already told him that they're not sure it will work. In that case, Tzahi will have to get another tube and bag and go on with the old arrangements, and who knows. . . .

Twenty-One

Then one night I wake up and see Yonatan standing beside me with a wheelchair. He stands there looking serious, not taking his eyes off me. His hair is fuzzy like a baby chick's but his eyes are like a lion cub's. I know that the time has come. He helps me get down into the chair, which is less difficult now: Felix worked so hard, and he's so obstinate, that it made my leg a lot stronger. I can already imagine myself walking straight, maybe with a little limp, but walking all right. The tourists won't be looking at me when I go down the market steps.

It's very late at night. A male nurse in the nurses' station is sleeping in the chair with his feet on the table. We sneak past him quietly. Yonatan leads and I follow. I ask myself how we're going to sneak past the guard at the end of the corridor on the way out, but instead of going toward the entrance Yonatan turns left to the hallway with the offices, and starts to look for a room in the dark. He walks up and down, as if searching for something. In the end he takes a tiny little flashlight out of his pocket. It's chained to a bunch of keys, and shines such a reddish light that I can't help wanting it for myself from the first moment. I never saw such a wonderful flashlight in all my life. Maybe it's the one I've always looked for in the garbage.

Yonatan unlocks the last door in the corridor with one of the keys in the bunch. He makes a sign for me to come in quietly. I roll in slowly on the rubber-covered wheels. I have no idea where we are going. If not through the gate, maybe he wants to go out the window? We're on a high floor in the building, but somebody planning to travel to outer space shouldn't be bothered by a few floors. We pass from one dark room to another and then another. Here we can have the overhead light on without being seen from the corridor. Yonatan turns on the light, and a smile lights his face. Then he goes to the window and closes the curtain, so no one will see us from outside.

There are two desks and few chairs in the room, a lamp, office papers. I don't see anything interesting here. Then Yonatan goes to a gadget that looks like a television standing on one of the desks and switches it on.

"Now look," he says.

I know — it's a computer. I saw one like it in the principal's room.

Yonatan takes a card out of his pajama pocket, not much bigger than a packet of cigarettes but flat. He pushes it into the computer and presses all kinds of buttons. Then something happens that I never saw in my life. The computer starts to play a magical tune, and the screen turns as blue as the sky, a sky more wonderful than the bluest sky I've ever seen, with silver and gold stars blinking on and off, winking at us, at me and Yonatan, in keeping with the music. Then burning suns pass before our eyes, and spaceships whiz off in all directions. I don't have time to see everything that's happening there. I want to say to Yonatan: Whoa there, slow down a bit — but I can't say a word. I slide the wheelchair closer to the computer and don't budge from there. I can't take my eyes off the screen, off this other world that Yonatan swims in like a fish in water, that freeness he talked about that I've never tasted before in my whole life.

Twenty-Two

"Which one are you, the blue boy or the green boy?" Yonatan asks.

I don't know what to say. On the screen the two boys are exactly the same: same size, same shape, only the color is different.

"The blue one . . . ?" I'm not sure.

"Then I'm the green one," says Yonatan. "It doesn't matter which one you choose, they're both made of the same stuff."

"Exactly?" I ask.

"All of us here on earth are made of the same materials. We all contain water, carbon, calcium, iron, protein, and some other stuff."

He looks at me and sees that I am amazed. Not that

I don't believe him, only that I never thought about it like this.

But it pleases him that I am amazed. He laughs. "All of us, Indians and French people, Africans and Russians, Jews and Arabs, Eskimos and Japanese — anyone you can think of!" He presses a button and the two of us, the blue boy and the green boy, get stuffed into spacesuits and begin to enter the spaceship.

"All the other living things on earth, they're also made up of the same materials, only arranged differently, that's all. Take camels, for example," Yonatan goes on.

"Camels?!"

"Or giraffes, elephants, butterflies, daffodils, olive trees, rabbits — everything is made up of the same mixture of materials, but in each one the mixture is organized a little differently. That's all. Now, you see this button? Press it."

I press. The doors of the spaceship slide shut. "Any time we want to see what's happening to us inside the spaceship, we'll press this button," he says, and presses a big red button.

The screen divides in two, and one corner shows the inside of the spaceship, with Yonatan and me sitting squashed together. There is no room to move a finger.

"Careful with my knee," I remind Yonatan.

He laughs. "Don't worry, your spacesuit will protect you." Then he shows me a lever that you need two hands to pull on. "You drive the spaceship," Yonatan tells me seriously. "Me, I can't do anything with my left hand. It won't be easy, but I'll help you as best I can. Space is full of objects. Watch out!"

And before I figure out where we are and where we are heading, Yonatan shouts: "Lift offff!" I hush him, or he'll wake the sleeping nurse. Now he tells me to grab the steering lever with both hands and whispers: "Five-Four-Three-Two-One-Zero . . . Go!!!" I pull the lever with both hands. A bright light floods the screen. For a moment it seems that the spaceship isn't moving. It's stuck to the ground. It's happy to stay down here. Or maybe it doesn't have the strength to rise up. But I pull on the lever with all my strength, and it begins to move. At first slowly, uncertainly. Then faster and faster, with a force that comes from I don't know where. It's being pulled to some faraway place. I feel as if I've let the giant genie out of the lamp, and now I have no control over anything. We're flying through space so fast that it makes me dizzy. But we're not alone here. All around us weird-looking lumps are whizzing past.

"Now the important thing is to avoid collisions!" Yonatan whispers to me, and I wiggle the spaceship between the lumps flying in our direction.

I'm confused. "What is all this?" I always thought that space was a lot emptier.

"We'll take a spin around our galaxy and then come back," says Yonatan, and presses all sorts of buttons.

We're flying among marvelous shining objects, and if I didn't have to avoid collisions I'd be happy to sit still for hours and do nothing but watch them passing before my eyes. In the distance I see necklaces of stars, and the stars flow through space, changing the shape of the necklaces in all kinds of wonderful arrangements, like the birds in the evening before it rains.

"What's over there?" I ask, pointing at the horizon.

"Those are galaxies that collided. The explosions that you see all the time are showing us in a few seconds what happens in space in two million years. Every star out there is influenced by the gravity of all the others, so they move about the whole time, drawing together and separating in strange and wonderful patterns. . . . Wait a moment! Now be careful,

careful!" Yonatan pulls my hand on the lever. I just manage to avoid hitting something that was flying toward us.

"This is a galaxy that likes to swallow up its neighbors."

"Dir balak — be careful!" I say to myself, maneuvering among all kinds of little bits flying wildly around us. "What are they?"

"They are asteroids, chunks of broken planets. Stars and planets are born and die, just like we do. They have a life of their own: childhood, old age, death."

"Childhood, old age, death? In these things?" I can't believe it.

"There, see those yellow ones — they are young stars, maybe fifty million years old or something. They are born from gas and dust. And over there, you see the glowing red ones? Those will die young."

"I didn't know that stars are also born and die . . . ," I mumbled.

"Sure they do!" says Yonatan. "Careful! You're not paying attention. We almost smashed into a comet. A collision with one of those would burn up our spaceship in a second!"

I'd always thought the sky was peaceful and calm.

Now I see that it's worse than a traffic jam at a road-block.

"We almost crashed," says Yonatan.

I'm sort of annoyed with myself that I didn't notice the comet.

"You have to be more careful," he says to me.

Now I'm feeling hurt. "It's easy for you to talk. I bet your dad showed you stars when you were still a baby."

We're traveling awfully fast through space. I try to avoid crashing into anything, so we won't burn up. I'm almost used to the speed. I'm starting to feel as if I've always been navigating among the stars.

"Here, in our solar system, all the planets had huge crashes in the past. Venus and Mars, and probably also our own Earth. Even the biggest planets, Jupiter and Saturn. But they didn't care, it hardly scratched them, they're so huge. Our spaceship is like a little nutshell among all these."

Dir balak! I warn myself.

"What's killing me," Yonatan goes on calmly, "is that the laws of physics work the same way all over the universe, and the chemistry is also the same every-where. Us and the stars, for example, are made of the same stuff."

"You and me?" I ask, laughing.

"Yes, you and me, Samir, we're made of star dust."

He laughs and I laugh. It's a nice idea, I think to myself.

Press a button — and we are back in our own galaxy, the one Yonatan calls the home galaxy. It's called the Milky Way. We'll soon be back in our own little solar system.

"Not that it's so little!" Yonatan says, excited. "In the whole universe, which is full of galaxies, it's something tiny, somewhere in the margins, but for us it's enormous. In fact, our dimensions and distances are suited to the planet Earth. They are not made for this vast universe. We've only just started to grasp the size of it in the last hundred years!"

"When are we going to reach Mars?" I ask. I'm a bit tired of this speed in space. I'd like to find me a fresh oasis with a few trees and take a break.

"In a little while," Yonatan assures me. "We could pop over to Venus. It's closer to our planet, but the trouble is, it's 380 degrees over there."

In that case, I'm not going to argue. I can wait until we get to Mars.

"You don't know how long I've been dreaming about Mars," Yonatan says in a soft voice. His skinny hand is patting the buttons. I try to listen to him, but I also have to look after the spaceship. So he shows me how to make it stop still a moment in space, just by pressing a button. I didn't know it could be done. At last I can rest a moment, thank God.

He looks at me and says, "You don't know what hopes I have about Mars. Ever since I was small, I've always hoped that there's life over there. I read books and talked about it endlessly with Dad. I bombarded him with questions. Nowadays they're not really expecting to find life on Mars. They've already landed two spaceships on it — *Viking One* and *Viking Two*. They took pictures and brought samples of sand and rocks, but they didn't find any signs of life. Maybe there are germs over there," he says sadly. "Maybe some kind of germs."

I know that's not what he was hoping for, this Yonatan. Not for germs.

We're approaching the planet Mars. I can see Yonatan getting excited. He wipes the sweat off his forehead with the back of his hand.

"Now hold tight!" he tells me. "With both hands! So we won't crash on landing. You know that landing this spaceship is a highly fateful moment . . . ?"

"How would I know?" I ask, annoyed again. "My

father doesn't work in the stars. I can tell you how the straight razor is stropped, and how much razor blades cost in every town in the West Bank."

"It's all right," Yonatan calms me down. "If the *Vikings* could land safely, why shouldn't we?"

"Who built that *Viking* spaceship, anyway?" I ask. I find that it helps to talk. I drive better that way.

Yonatan explains, "It's hard to say who built it, because in every scientific discovery there are tens of thousands of people involved. And we mustn't forget the scientists of past generations. We wouldn't have gotten this far without their discoveries. Anyhow, in 1976 we got to the point that we could land *Viking* on Mars — a hundred million kilometers from Earth. Just think about it!" That's how he talks, this kid, as if he and his father were the ones who landed that *Viking*, or whatever it's called, on Mars. "It's because *Viking* has been to Mars that we know an awful lot more about it today than we used to know. Careful!"

Now the talk between me and Yonatan becomes fast and sounds like pilots' talk, something I saw in a series about the war that American pilots were in, only they spoke English.

Me: "What happened?"

Yonatan: "We've got to think carefully where we want to land."

Me: "Why?"

Yonatan: "Because there are many volcanoes and all kinds of stormy and peculiar places. Let's land in Utopia."

Me: "Where's that?"

Yonatan: "That's the place where the *Vikings* landed."

Me: "All right, direct me!"

Yonatan: "Change the angle of the lever. I'll try to locate the site."

Me: "How do I do that?"

Yonatan: "You bend the lever a little to the left."

Me: "What now?"

Yonatan: "Now — don't you see?"

Me: "Where?"

Yonatan: "There, directly below us, that's Utopia!"

Me: "Right, I'm pulling a bit to the left."

Yonatan: "Great. Just a little bit more. Now! *Now!*"

Again he's yelling at me as if all my life I've done nothing but land spaceships on planets. I'm getting jumpy again. Maybe I'll end up like my grandpa. A short-tempered type. I'll start pinching cheeks too.

Yonatan: "Now! Now!"

Me: "What do I do now?"

Yonatan: "Lift the lever! Quickly!"

What do you know. It's a miracle. We land on this reddish planet. I can't believe it. Our spaceship is standing upright on the sand and is starting to stick out its legs. I could kiss the dust under its feet, as Grandpa would say.

"We're lucky that we're even more advanced than *Viking*," Yonatan says, beaming all over. "We are fortunate — we don't have to stay stuck here on these legs. We can put out ratchet wheels and move around on Mars like a tractor."

Yonatan presses a green button and special wheels with teeth come out on all sides of the spaceship, like arms. I press the button that shows the inside of the spaceship, and there are Yonatan and me, the blue boy and the green boy, laughing at us from inside their spacesuits. I can hear faraway music and thousands of stars all around wink on and off to the beat.

"We've moved to Level Two," Yonatan says, pleased.

"How about going outside?" I ask, stretching myself. "It's crowded in here."

"It's not so easy," he says. "We'd better move about on the wheels and tour around the place. The temperature outside is 50 degrees below zero. At night it can go down to 100 below zero. We do have good space-suits, but we should look around a while before going outside. Also, there's not enough oxygen in the air and too many ultraviolet rays from the sun, because this planet doesn't have an ozone layer, like planet Earth."

"Our planet is quite well made, then," I now realize.

"That's what I always say," Yonatan smiles. "Or my father says."

So I grip the steering lever and we roll along slowly. All around us are sands. Field after field, all of sand. Sometimes the fields are covered with small rocks, as if somebody scattered stones everywhere. I see high mountains in the distance. It's so strange that I'm driving around on Mars. So far away from Earth. And here we are, traveling freely on this red-brown ground that is only ours. Here nobody can stop you and demand your identity card. Over among the mountains I see a wadi.

"I'm turning to that wadi," I say to Yonatan.

He laughs. "In a minute you'll see what kind of wadi it is. You know, there's a canyon in America, called the Grand Canyon, my mother wrote me about it, like a deep crack between mountains. On earth it's considered huge. But this little wadi on Mars can swallow it up, and three more like it. This wadi here is three thousand miles long. You can travel along it forever and never reach the end.

And what do you know — we move nearer, and the whole screen is filled with a huge, long wadi. Suddenly Yonatan presses a button and the door of the spaceship opens.

"We've got to see this close up," he says, so we step outside.

At long last — after being cooped up during the whole journey. I straighten my knee carefully. I'm walking fine. I don't limp here at all. We walk to the wadi, Yonatan and me. We're about the size of little black flyspecks.

"The Mariner's Valley," says Yonatan. We stand there together overlooking the valley in complete silence. It's impossible to speak. We've never seen anything so beautiful in our lives, not even imagined such a thing. We stand there saying nothing for a long time. I don't know what Yonatan is thinking. My thoughts are all confused, like a strong whirlpool. In the end, Yonatan speaks.

"Listen, Samir," he says, "if we're fed up with our world, if there are troubles over there and we don't feel good, we can always come here, to this other world."

"But how?" I ask. "You say yourself that it's cold here and there's no ozone and not enough oxygen or anything."

"Planet Earth wasn't so great in the beginning," he replies. "Today we can learn from the way our planet developed, and make improvements on other planets."

"Improvements?" I really don't understand this kid at all. How can you improve the universe?

"Listen carefully!" Yonatan says seriously, passing his hand as he always does through his yellow hair. I'm freezing in 50 below zero, but he's sweating. His hair stands up like a hedgehog's prickles. He looks so excited. I realize that all the days that we spent lying in Room Six, and all the hours I was in the operation, Yonatan was waiting for this moment. He begins to press buttons and improve the planet Mars. "First of all, we'll dig trenches from the Pole and bring water to the dry, sandy areas. Water is the most basic thing. Water is life."

He presses a button and little blue streams begin to flow quietly through the sand hills.

"Now oxygen," Yonatan says, dead serious. He presses another button and little seedlings pop up and creep on the ground along the streams, little fleshy cactuses. "These don't need a lot of water. They store it," he explains.

"Where did the seedlings come from?" I ask suspiciously.

"We brought them from Earth," Yonatan grins. "We brought plants that don't need a lot of care, and they'll increase the amount of oxygen in the air. Later, other plants will develop from them."

The plants begin to grow and cover the banks of the streams. I try my luck and press a button too. Here and there woods begin to appear on the hills. I like that. I make them thicker. I seem to hear the first birds chirping among the trees.

"Wait, what about those rays you mentioned?"

But Yonatan has an answer for every question. He has thought of everything. "We'll pour in some gas that will hang over the planet like clouds, and serve as a curtain between us and the sun."

I'm not sure. "You think it will work? If we don't sort out the business with the rays, the creatures won't stand a chance here." I'm getting to be like Yonatan, talking like a great scientist.

"So let's say it's a temporary solution," Yonatan suggests. "Later on we can develop something better."

Clouds begin to thicken over the planet and turn into a kind of curtain between the sun and the ground.

"Yonatan," I say, "how about we make . . . you know . . . among all the other improvements, couldn't we also make a sea?"

"What do we need a sea for?" he asks.

I don't know how to explain it to him. Maybe it won't help to develop Mars, but I must have it. I'm ashamed to tell him that I've never seen the sea. Yonatan looks at all the buttons. Then he takes out a computer handbook and begins to read through it.

"How about a lake?" he says finally, his nose in the book.

"Will it look like the sea?" I ask, full of hope.

"A freshwater lake will be more useful to us now," Yonatan says, very thoughtful.

"Okay, but a great big lake so you can't see the other side," I beg.

We play with the buttons and consult together and try all kinds of experiments. We get the start of a river, but not in the place we intended. It's too close to a volcano, one that the book tells Yonatan still erupts sometimes. It spits out a red fire called lava, throwing this lava up to amazing heights. We pass from screen to screen. Each screen shows a different part of the planet.

In the end we find a flat sandy valley that looks quiet enough, and we start to bring the water into it. I make the lake bigger and bigger. Yonatan thinks it's quite big enough, but I can't stop. I want it to spread as far as the horizon. I want it to be unlimited, so no one will see the end of it. Yonatan is already planning to bring frozen fishes from Earth and thaw them here, but on the condition that it will be forbidden to fish or to hunt in our world. The fishes will be able to live a long, peaceful life.

Suddenly I don't need to go any farther. I can stand here, on the shore of the lake, and know that everything is possible. I understand Yonatan's big secret. Something is happening to me tonight, something wonderful that never happened to me with anybody. Not even with Fadi, my brother, the boy who grew up with me and who was my closest buddy.

I'm standing here with Yonatan on the shore of a blue lake, remembering how we went out in the evening, Fadi and me, to the yard to bury the rabbit. It was raining. We stood beside the hole and Fadi wrapped her in a newspaper, so she wouldn't get wet. He put her in the hole and then laid the chocolate in the corner, near her head, and we both shoveled the muddy earth over her and covered everything.

But even then, when we stood together in the rain for a few minutes, saying nothing, even then we weren't as close as Yonatan and I are close now. Maybe because the most important thing we had between us, Fadi and me, was what we buried in the ground. There was nothing left. Nothing with which to carry on.

Now, for the first time, I think that maybe that's what killed Fadi. That's why he didn't have the strength to run fast and get away. That's what killed him — that he didn't have anything to carry on with. With Dad who stopped talking to us some time ago, and Mom who works as a cleaner then spends the night in the bakery, and is always tired, and Bassam who disappeared to Kuwait so as to send some money, and Grandpa shrinking from day to day on account of the cigarettes.

"I want to say a few words to my brother Fadi who is dead," I say to Yonatan. "I wasn't at his funeral." He falls silent, the green boy. He moves a few steps back and leaves the blue boy alone with the lake. The air stands still. There is complete silence all around. On this planet only Yonatan and I are breathing, and maybe a few germs. I don't know if there is wind. Hard to tell. The woods we grew are on the other side of the mountains. The lake looks smooth.

"Fadi," I say, "you were a precious stone, you were a lion cub. . . . I didn't put chocolate in the ground for you. I wasn't even at the funeral, if you must know. If I'd come with all the mourners and wailing women, you wouldn't have heard me anyway. Forgive me, Fadi, but I hate funerals. Honestly, Fadi, I didn't know you were still outside in the street, and when Adnan told me to run away, I didn't think. And sometimes I even forget to remember you. I want you to know that. Also, that I got off the windowsill. But at night under the blanket I think about you. And today, here on Mars, I understand: You had no way of carrying on. . . ."

I stand here on the shore of the blue lake that we've made, Yonatan and me, my friend from the Jewish hospital. We're improving a new world, free from troubles. Nothing looks impossible to us, now that we're together.

Twenty-Three

Today I'm going home. That's what they call it here. Even if you live far away and have to travel home by bus, they don't say you're traveling home. They say "going home," as if it's walking distance from the hospital.

In the morning Vardina said to Felix, "Samir is going home today. We have to help him pack and prepare his discharge letter." I love the way she says it. She waters the plants and sings her song, but today she isn't looking at the plant. She's looking at me. Going home, that's like saying you were good. Like saying you've won.

I like it when they say about me "He's going home." As if I'm like everyone else. I love a lot of the words they use here. I love it when Yonatan says "m.p.h." It sounds so fine: "Some galaxies are flying away from us at a speed of two hundred em-pee-aitch. . . ." What a sentence. Sometimes I repeat it to myself under the blanket. They sound like good words to use against the evil eye. Maybe I'll exchange "Once there was a wizard . . ." for one of these sentences.

For instance, when Felix tells Vardina, "I gave Ludmilla ten cee-cee of the medication . . ." Or when a green nurse in a mask says to me, just like on television: "When you wake up, Samir, the operation will be behind you. . . ."

I don't know what it is about these sentences. I only have to repeat them and I'm far away. I'm home, but with these sentences in my mind. They're just mine. Nobody, not Mom or Dad or Nawar or Grandpa, not Bassam or Adnan — nobody's ever heard these sentences. I was in the Jews' hospital. That's all they know about me. But me — my mind is full of words, voices. Felix's goat face, the balloons he pulls out of ears, the lakes on the walls, Yonatan, the planet Mars, and our own real lake over there, a million times more beautiful than any other lake . . . I shouldn't say it, but it's as if I had another family for a while. Something secret. I can't explain it to anybody. Maybe I'll be a completely different Samir from what I used to be. In my heart. Only Tzahi's words, the way they sounded, will stay even now outside my heart.

I sit in the waiting room with my medical file, waiting. In the morning there was a phone call from the village to say that Dad closed the shop and spent three days waiting in line outside the Administration with a letter from the hospital till they finally gave him a permit to come and pick me up. They didn't know what time he'd be here. It all depends on the roadblocks and the soldiers and the situation and the buses. I don't know what else. Now there's no traffic coming from that district. It's all under "closure."

I can hardly believe that my village is still where it was, in the same place. And if there's a curfew there, I'll be thinking of Ingrid One and Ingrid Two and waiting to hear them come in with tea and cookies. And when I lie in my bed at night I'll hear Felix coming in to make sure I'm off to the Land of Nod.

Suddenly I see Tzahi wandering in the hallway. He passes me by again and again without looking at me. But I see him, whether I like it or not. And he doesn't look the way he always does, this Tzahi. I know him.

Even if he's not part of the family, I know every

movement that he makes, every fold in his pajamas. That's how it is when you spend a long time together in the same room with someone. You can't help it. But now his pajamas don't look the same. There's something missing. I don't know what. Tzahi looks thinner, or something. His body looks unusual. Not the same as always. But what I notice most is that he's acting like something special happened to him today.

He's walking around, smiling to himself, and isn't saying "Cool!" every minute. I don't care. I look away. But Tzahi wants me to look in his direction. Yes. He comes closer and closer. He's trying to force me to look at him. He runs past me and rushes to the end of the hallway, stands near the elevator, and whistles to himself. Why should I look at him? So what if he's whistling? I look at him. Just out of curiosity. I don't care. I'm going home, and he's staying here. I won. Why shouldn't I look at him?

Tzahi makes me a little sign with his hand. I'm not sure why, but he goes on. He's staying put beside the elevator and keeps signaling to me with his hand. I'm sure he means me. There's nobody but us in the waiting room, just me and him. So I get up, don't know why. What have I got to lose? I get up and limp toward him. As I walk, I remember what Felix kept telling me: "You've got two legs, and they're both the same. One's a bit weak, but it's just as usable as the other. What have you got the leg for? To walk on. If you take pity on it, this leg will take it into its head that it's sick. . . ." That kind of talk.

I go up to Tzahi. Not too close. I stand a little way from him and pretend I'm looking at the elevator. Waiting for Dad to come out of it. Tzahi starts to walk down the hallway. I guess he didn't mean any-thing. But no — he makes a sign for me to follow. So I follow him. What do I care? I've got to walk a lot, Felix said. Walk as much as possible.

Tzahi reaches the end of the hallway and stops. He's looking back, to see if I'm coming. I stop be-side one of those pictures with lakes, and look at the water. I'm thinking, maybe it's a kind of game. A kind of game I don't know. But I've got to be careful. Any game with this Tzahi could end up in the snake pit. I have to take it step by step. Always leave a way out. I've never played this kind of game.

In the curfews we used to play with bugs, Fadi and me. We had nothing to do, so we'd get a couple of black bugs and put them into two bottles. Then we'd lay the bottles on the ground, each with his bottle, and whoever had the bug that found the exit first, won. I don't know why Fadi's bug always won. Every time. Mine used to get stuck inside. Allah alone knows what it was thinking about. Sometimes it even went right up to the opening, my bug, then stopped still like it was paralyzed, like it was thinking hard. I'd try to cheer it on, whisper to it from the mouth of the bottle: "Come, little beauty. Come, sister, see what a pretty world there is outside the bottle!" But the bug acted like it was in detention. Like Allah had already lost it.

Then Nawar would come and sweep the room till we got dizzy. She always thought the room was getting cleaner, but she only raised dust. She gave us hell about our games, said we were bringing in dirt. She chose the most exciting moment to crowd us with her broom. Now I'm glad for Fadi that his bugs always won. I'm glad he had those good moments.

Tzahi suddenly pulls down his pajama pants and pees into the big potted plant standing at the end of the hallway. I don't get it at first. I just look around to see if anybody is coming. Tzahi is peeing, looking back at me and smiling. It's not his usual smile. It's not sly or naughty. Just a smile of somebody who's pleased to pieces. Then, all at once, it hits me: They took off the bag and took out the tube. And it worked! Everything's okay with him. Tzahi is showing me that everything is okay with him.

The elevator stops and Tzahi quickly pulls up his pants and goes away. Again he turns his head and signs me to follow. So I follow. I say to myself, why are you limping after him like an idiot, hey, Samir? But I can't help it. I've got to see what he'll do next.

We reach the X ray department. It's still early and there's no line, only a couple of old men sitting near the door, looking at us when we pass by. They look at Tzahi, then at me. They don't miss a thing. Tzahi stops at the corner. He stands in front of another big potted plant but isn't doing anything. He's waiting for me. I slow down and he makes a sign with his hand, smiling all the time. So I limp over to the end of the corridor till I catch up with him, and he looks at me, giggling. I hope he's not going to do it here, with the two old guys sitting there, looking at us. But he is. He's gone nuts, this boy. I see him reaching for his pants. "Dir balak!" the words slip out of my mouth. "Careful!" For a moment I feel the way I do with Adnan. Exactly the same.

Now Tzahi is really tickled pink. He can't help himself. He's like a baby. He has to do it here too. And he gives me a friendly nod: "You too . . . ," it says. Maybe this is where I fall into the pit. Allah only knows.

It's exactly the same as with Adnan. You know how a thing starts, but you've no idea how it's going to finish. I'm not so crazy that I'll start peeing in potted plants, in a hospital, and at the Jews' hospital too. But this smile on Tzahi's face. I know in my heart that it's a new smile. Suddenly, I don't want him to think I'm chicken, this Tzahi.

"The old guys . . . ," I whisper. As if everything would be all right if the old guys weren't sitting here.

"What will they do?" Tzahi whispers back. "Call the police . . . ?" He can't help giggling. "Come, both of us . . . ," he says. I never heard him speak in such a voice. Asking for something. Almost begging. Come, both of us. I love this sentence. The smile sits deep inside his eyes. But the smile isn't begging, only tempting. Exactly like Adnan. "Don't be chicken . . . ," Adnan says to me.

I think to myself, You won't be able to undo your pants. It's more difficult for you — you're not in pajamas. Tzahi stares at me as if hypnotized. But I'm paralyzed. I can't move.

Just then a male nurse comes by, pushing a bed, and we both dash off along the corridor. Tzahi runs ahead, laughing, and I limp behind him. At the end he stops and turns to see if I'm coming. I think suddenly that we've come too far, and that maybe Dad has already arrived. Maybe he's waiting for me even now. I've got to go. But Tzahi comes back and puts his arm around my shoulder and we keep going, without a word, till we reach the stairs and go down into the courtyard.

Tzahi goes on and I go with him. For weeks we've lain in the same room and never exchanged a good word. Now suddenly, in a few seconds, it's all been wiped clean. I'd like to have a little bit of anger left, but there isn't any. Maybe I am too soft. Maybe I still haven't learned what Dad says to us from time to time: "Don't be so tough you'll break, and don't be so soft you'll be crushed." Maybe I am a coward. I must try to be brave. Not to be a follower. To be stubborn as a mule. Yes, I'll repeat this to myself, and maybe in the end I'll be trained. But maybe I also need to keep a curl from the hair of a wanted man, like Nawar does.

But I don't need it for lovey-dovey nonsense. I need it to remind me to be a man.

We reach the sandbox and stand in front of it together. I'm not afraid, there's only a nice feeling. And curiosity. We're alone in this courtyard and I see what Tzahi is going to do now. And what I will do too. Tzahi lowers his pajama pants a little, and his eyes smile at me. Without knowing why, I undo my pants. It takes longer than pajamas. Tzahi waits patiently, and as soon as I'm ready, as if on command, both of us, Tzahi and me, pee together into the sand.

We stand here together, peeing. The air is still. Just like when I said my last good-bye to Fadi on the planet Mars. It's quiet in the courtyard. Not a leaf stirs. At such moments maybe the wind itself holds its breath. Only the sun is stroking us quietly. The kids in the ward upstairs gather in the windows and laugh. We're also laughing, but it's a different sort of laugh. I don't know what Tzahi is thinking about now. Me, under the laugh, I'm already thinking about home, and how I'll want to remember this moment and won't believe that it happened, but I'll want to believe it. Because it's so simple. I'll want to believe that I, Samir, a boy from the occupied West Bank, stood here with a Jewish boy who has a soldier brother, and the two of us peed into a sandbox and laughed and didn't give a damn about the whole world. Yes . . . every day I'll have to search for some new sign that will remind me that it all really happened, and was not a dream.

Glossary

dinar: Jordanian currency; formerly a gold coin in use throughout the Muslim world

kinnar: a spice-flavored tea

knafeh: a sweet pastry made of semolina

labaneh: a yogurt cheese, formed into balls and kept in olive oil

mastaba: a window seat built into the wall

muezzin: a man who calls Muslims to prayer from the top of a minaret, or mosque tower

narghile: a pipe used for smoking tobacco through water

Palestine: Geographic Palestine is the region bounded by Lebanon, the Sinai Peninsula, the Mediterranean Sea, and the Jordan River. The Arab inhabitants of this land are known as Palestinians. The state of Israel came into being in 1948, on about half of the land of geographic Palestine. The remainder was ruled by Jordan and Egypt. These territorial divisions later changed because of the Arab-Israeli wars.

Ramadan: the ninth month of the Islamic year, observed as
    sacred, with fasting practiced daily from sunrise to sunset
sahlab: a sweet milky drink or pudding
shekel: the unit of currency used in Israel
schnitzel: a breaded chicken cutlet
Territories, or *Occupied Territories*: land captured by Israel
    from neighboring Arab states in the June War of 1967,
    including the West Bank with East Jerusalem, the Gaza
    Strip with the Sinai Peninsula, and the Syrian Golan Heights.
    From 1988 to 1991 Palestinians on the West Bank and in
    Gaza actively resisted the occupation — a movement known
    as the intifada, or "uprising." This was followed by a series
    of negotiations concerning the future of the Territories,
    which have continued intermittently since 1994.
Thousand and One Nights, or *Arabian Nights*: A classic of world
    literature containing medieval stories from throughout
    the Arab and Muslim world, collected into one long,
    linked narrative. Among the many stories are *Scheherazade,
    Sinbad, Harun al-Rashid, Aladdin,* and *Ali Baba and the Forty
    Thieves*.
UNRWA: United Nations Relief and Works Agency
wadi: the bed or valley of a stream in regions of southwestern
    Asia and northern Africa that is usually dry, except during
    the rainy season, when it often forms an oasis.
yarmulke: a skullcap worn especially by religious Jewish males
"*Yiboneh bais hamikdosh bimheira beyomainu:*" a wish for the
    rebuilding of the Temple of Zion. The Hebrew translates
    to: "The Temple shall be built speedily and in our lifetime."

About this Scholastic Signature Author

DANIELLA CARMI was hailed by *Publishers Weekly* as one of the most talented Israeli authors writing today. She was born in Tel Aviv, and now lives in Jerusalem. She has three children.

About the Translator

YAEL LOTAN has translated many other novels and nonfiction books into English, most recently *Persian Brides* by Dorit Rabinyan, which won the Jewish Quarterly Wingate Literary Prize. Ms. Lotan lives in Israel.